MURDER IN THE CHRISTMAS MARKET

A CLAIRE BASKERVILLE MYSTERY BOOK 9

SUSAN KIERNAN-LEWIS

SAN MARCO PRESS

No place sparkles like Paris at Christmas time—complete with roaring fire, a little mistletoe and a touch of murder. When expat and private detective Claire Baskerville sets out to make this year's holiday the most memorable one yet, she hadn't counted on tripping over a dead body virtually on her doorstep. The charming array of Christmas market booths that line the Champs Elysées is the setting for this holiday whodunit that will have you reaching for a hot mulled wine in between gasps of shock.

This season, step into the Christmas spirit *à Paris* and get ready to enjoy the magic—and the shiver!—with this page-turning Christmas mystery.

Books by Susan Kiernan-Lewis
The Maggie Newberry Mysteries
Murder in the South of France
Murder à la Carte
Murder in Provence
Murder in Paris
Murder in Aix
Murder in Nice
Murder in the Latin Quarter
Murder in the Abbey
Murder in the Bistro
Murder in Cannes
Murder in Grenoble
Murder in the Vineyard
Murder in Arles
Murder in Marseille
Murder in St-Rémy
Murder à la Mode
Murder in Avignon
Murder in the Lavender

Savannah is Burning

The Stranded in Provence Mysteries
Parlez-Vous Murder?
Crime and Croissants
Accent on Murder
A Bad Éclair Day
Croak, Monsieur!
Death du Jour
Murder Très Gauche
Wined and Died
Murder, Voila!
A French Country Christmas
Fromage to Eternity
Crepe Expectations

The Irish End Games
Free Falling
Going Gone
Heading Home
Blind Sided
Rising Tides
Cold Comfort
Never Never
Wit's End
Dead On
White Out
Black Out
End Game

The Mia Kazmaroff Mysteries
Reckless
Shameless

Breathless
Heartless
Clueless
Ruthless

Ella Out of Time
Swept Away
Carried Away
Stolen Away

1

The scent of pine mixing with that of just-baked cookies gave the apartment the perfect feel of Christmas. I stood at the living room window of my eighth arrondissement Parisian apartment and stared out as the snowflakes drifted lazily downward. If I hadn't just put my young foster son Robbie to bed—which was getting harder and harder the closer we got to the big day—I would have pointed it out to him. As it was, I decided if the snow stuck, he could happily lose his mind over it in the morning.

"More rum, *chérie*?"

I turned to see my downstairs neighbor and dearest friend Geneviève standing in the doorway to the kitchen with a bottle of Rhum Clement in her hand. We'd been hitting the hot buttered toddies pretty solidly ever since I'd declared my holiday shopping mostly done.

"I'm good," I said with a wobbly laugh.

This wasn't my first Christmas in Paris—I've lived here for nearly four years after all—but it qualified as being my strangest yet. Part of that was because I'd broken up with my longtime boyfriend over the summer and I continued to be estranged from my only child, my daughter Catherine. It was also strange this year because it was my granddaughter's first Christmas and because she lived with me, I would have the pleasure of introducing her to the magic of the season.

Geneviève came into the living room with her own hot buttered rum and sat down.

"You are getting *la nostalgie, chérie*?" she asked, cocking an eyebrow at me.

Geneviève who was in her mid-eighties was the quintessential French woman. She was slender, with impeccable style and perfect skin, her silver hair always beautifully coifed in a French twist that accentuated her long neck.

"No," I said. "I'm just imagining how happy Robbie will be when he wakes up to the winter wonderland tomorrow."

"I am sorry that Catherine will not come this Christmas, *chérie*."

Geneviève always could read me so well.

"It's probably for the best," I said although even someone much less dense than Geneviève could tell that was a lie.

"Yes, well, it might be problematic," she said taking a sip of her drink, "since you still have not mentioned to her that she has a daughter."

I grimaced at her bluntness. How could Catherine have no idea that she has a daughter? Well, that's a long story of stolen frozen eggs that I successfully tracked down last summer in Dubai until I ended up with a bundle of joy— my biological granddaughter—placed in my arms.

And now, for reasons that sounded good only to me, Catherine still didn't know.

She was totally unaware of the existence of little Maddie. Her daughter.

"I was intending to tell her if she came for Christmas," I said. "These things should be said face to face."

"Coward."

I'd heard it before from Geneviève. As far as she was concerned, I should have told Catherine months ago. But you know how that goes. The longer you wait, the worse it gets, and the longer you wait.

"You are absolutely correct," I assured her, mostly just to end the discussion. "Hey, I think I changed my mind about the rum." I stood up and held out my hand for her cup.

As I went to the kitchen to warm up the butter and water on the stove in a saucepan, I found myself thinking of Jean-Marc again. We'd had our ups and downs over the years—the first time I met him he arrested me for the murder of my husband!—but he was always someone I felt I could trust (well, after I made bail anyway). Our breach this time felt permanent. I'd been the one to break with him, but I'd done something unforgivable that had resulted in him quitting his job with the Paris police department.

After giving it long thought, I could see how he might have felt he couldn't do anything else but retire and I kick myself for not realizing he might have reacted that way. My only defense was that I was going through an awful lot during that time—*may I please take this time to reference the hunt and discovery of my granddaughter Maddie?*—and I wasn't able to pick up on all the emotional clues from him that I should have.

While I've since come to my senses, Jean-Marc, rightly so, is uninterested in hearing my in-person apologies. I do not blame him. And I understand why he blames me.

That doesn't mean it hurts any less or that I miss him

any less.

I returned to the living room with the hot toddies and saw the snow outside the window coming down even harder now.

"Goodness," I said, handing Geneviève her mug, "I hope this means I'm not going to be obligated to dig out the sled tomorrow."

While at sixty-four I am perfectly capable of pulling my four-year-old foster son up and down the boulevard Haussmann I didn't relish the inevitable reliance on ice packs and ibuprofen I'd be dependent on afterward. The fact was, I have a perfectly wonderful sitter who has been my savior with both Robbie and Maddie, but she was on a school break ski trip with her friends.

I sat down and gazed into the crackling blaze on the hearth. Christmas carols played in the background on my HomePod. With the warmth of the hot rum in my system and the fragrance of the cookies Geneviève and I had baked today still hanging in the air, I felt that—in spite of everything—it was going to be a blessed and perfect Christmas.

My phone dinged on the coffee table in front of me.

"Don't answer it, *chérie*," Geneviève said.

I'm a private investigator here in Paris and while I'd wrapped up as many cases as I could before the holidays, I did have one or two that still required my attention.

"You know you can't say that to a mother," I told Geneviève, although the chance that Catherine was texting me was low and we both knew it.

I picked up on my phone and read and reread the text.

"Who is it, *chérie*?" Geneviève asked, leaning over my shoulder to look for herself.

"It's Jean-Marc," I said with a hushed surprise in my voice. "He wants to meet for a drink."

2

_____

Guy felt the heat flush through his tense and rigid body as he pounded down the stairs of his apartment, each step seeming to pump more anger into him. He reached the foyer and flung open the wrought-iron security door, taking some satisfaction as he heard the loud discordant clang it made against the wall.

The night air raked his lungs and he inhaled sharply as if to punish himself.

For believing him! For trusting him!

He bolted into the street, forcing a couple to step off the wet sidewalk to avoid him. Inane holiday decorations bobbed in the cold night breeze overhead. Colored lights blinked obscenely at the edge of the awning on the corner café. At the moment he hated everyone who felt happy or merry or wanted to celebrate Christmas.

He ground his teeth as he pushed forward, scowling at yet another seemingly happy couple on the sidewalk ahead of him.

Bastard! Let him rot in hell! But by God she would rot with him!

He turned down the stretch that led to the rue Brunel and finally the Champs-Élysées, his anger amping up with every step. Everywhere he looked he was surrounded by cheerful, dazzling, twinkling lights, boughs of fir and wreaths of holly. He wished he could take a match to the lot of it!

And him.

The man who'd betrayed him. The man who'd built him up only to destroy him in the end.

Guy jammed his hand into his pocket to touch the handle of the gun. He felt his vision blur. Tonight he felt more confident than he ever had before.

Tonight, someone was going to pay for what had been done to him.

3

Pomme stamped her feet from behind the counter of the kiosk. Her boss Monsieur Omar had agreed to provide a space heater, but it was an old one and didn't warm the space behind the counter so much as burn the backs of her legs. Even as cold as she was, she kept moving away from the heater.

Pomme knew she shouldn't complain. She was glad to have the job. Even with cleaning offices and making *crêpes* in the Latin Quarter, without the mulled wine kiosk gig there would be no extra money for Christmas—not since Pierre had left her.

The tinny sound of Christmas carols filtered down the aisle between the wooden chalets where passersby walked.

Pomme had read that over a million light bulbs were draped in four hundred trees up and down the Champs-Élysées this Christmas. Watching them as they twinkled magically, she couldn't help but feel her heart swell. An hour ago, she had seen one of several horse-drawn carriages clip-clop past her stall with the rosy-cheeked faces of two little children bundled up between their parents. That had squeezed her heart.

She straightened up the displays of wine bottles, packaged candies and cellophane-wrapped gingerbread on the counter. People only came for the hot mulled wine, but she had to admit that the cookies made the kiosk look more festive. She'd put a little plastic Christmas tree with blinking lights in the back shelf of the kiosk, and that helped too. The front of the booth was decorated with fake snow and fake greenery with fake holly balls. Gaudy tinsel in silver and gold draped in lopsided swags from the front. It seemed to Pomme that Monsieur Omar had envisioned a German lebkuchen stand instead of a French mulled wine stand, or maybe he just got the kiosk cheap and it had come this way.

The tourists didn't seem to mind. Wearing scarves and brightly colored knit caps, they ambled past. The irresistible scent of mulled wine with cloves and orange slices drifted out into the street and collared them as they walked by. All the other kiosks sold hot wine too in addition to roasted chestnuts, burnt peanuts, and gingerbread.

Pomme thought of her two little ones at home and how excited they were for *Père Noël*'s visit. She reminded herself that she'd need to visit Monoprix tomorrow to pick up the little action figures she knew they wanted. By her calculations, she could just afford them if she signed up for another shift at the *crêpe* stand in the fifth arrondissement. She'd have to do it on the Saturday before Christmas—and she still had no childcare—but she was hoping an answer would come to her in the meantime. Her boys were good children and mostly well-behaved, but they were boys and she had nightmares about them drinking cleaning products or burning the apartment down. She'd had to quit cable months ago when Patrick left.

She rubbed the ache in her lower back. It was always there now. She couldn't rest enough to make it go away these days. Maybe after the holidays were over.

She smiled at a couple who walked slowly by her kiosk but who never made eye contact with her.

Maybe after she'd given the boys a good Christmas—*somehow*—she could pull back on all the extra jobs.

She was just so tired.

4

I hurried to the café that Jean-Marc had suggested for our rendezvous. It was off the Champs-Élysées but close enough that I could see the famous avenue awash in blinking fairy lights from the Arc de Triumph all the way to the Place de la Concord. It sat under a canopy of leafless trees—each draped with twinkling lights that spanned the street in a glittering display of the season. The very air around me smelled of cinnamon and ginger and pine...and possibilities.

I was early so I seated myself at table and ordered a coffee. I'd had enough alcohol for tonight and wanted to be alert for my reunion with Jean-Marc. This really was the best Christmas present I could imagine if Jean-Marc had found his way to forgiving me for my behavior last summer.

I had so many things to ask him: How was he doing? What was he was doing for a living? Had he missed me?

Geneviève had been happy to turn on the television and stay with the kids while I met with Jean-Marc. She was another reason for me to be grateful. I couldn't do my life—

raising two children at my age in a foreign country—without her.

And if it turns out I have a chance of getting back together with Jean-Marc—I scolded myself for getting ahead of myself. Taking in a long breath, I sipped my coffee and shivered in my heavy wool coat. The snow had slowed a bit now. It was cold enough so I had no doubts about it still being on the ground when Robbie woke up in the morning.

Maybe Jean-Marc would be willing to go to the park with me and Robbie tomorrow? If so, I could bundle up Maddie and bring her too. Robbie was crazy about Jean-Marc and had been none too happy when I told him he wouldn't be seeing him again.

Even at this hour—it was nearly eleven o'clock—there were people rushing past the café and stopping in. It was a bit late for dinner—even for the French—but the bustle of so many people, wearing colorful knit scarves and leather boots, their cheeks rosy from the cold, instilled in me a feeling of goodwill. I'd noticed, however much of it was a fantasy on my part, that people seemed to be acting more benevolent and generous the last couple of weeks. I loved hearing them greet each other with a happy "Joyeux Noël!"

I ordered a second coffee and sternly told myself to slow down. It was all very well to be alert but at this rate I'd be shaking if I didn't watch the caffeine intake. As it was, I was sure I'd have trouble sleeping tonight. But I didn't care.

I was being given a second chance by Jean-Marc. A chance to explain my behavior last summer—which was very defensible—but to apologize for it too. Jean-Marc was a special man and like none I'd ever been with before. But he was also in many ways typical for a man in that he had his pride and as much as he loved me, being shown up by me—

especially in front of his own precinct—had been difficult to endure.

I'd made it worse by haranguing him over it. True, I'd been nervous and half hysterical with fear that I wouldn't find Maddie, but that didn't erase the words I'd said to him —emasculating, hurtful words.

I glanced at my watch and saw that I'd been sitting here nearly forty minutes. Out of the corner of my eye I saw the waiters begin to stack tables and chairs on the terrace and wheel the standing propane heat lamps into the café interior.

I pulled out my phone. There was no text from him. With a feeling of foreboding, I texted him.

<Im here. Are you near?>

I watched as the corresponding bubbles showed up that typically indicated someone was crafting a response.

I watched as the bubbles stopped. And no reply came.

I felt a slow heaviness settle into my chest.

I signaled the waiter for my bill. Jean-Marc had left his job at the Paris homicide division—a job he'd held for nearly thirty years and one he loved. Leaving that job, voluntary or not, had been a terrible loss for him. It wouldn't be solved with one outreach, no matter how premature it now seemed to be.

I paid my bill and gathered up my purse, feeling the chill of the night air all the way through my coat as I made my way into the street for the cold, cold walk home.

5

———

The snow had started back up in earnest.

It was just as well, Pomme thought, shivering. There had only been one customer in the last hour and none in the past thirty minutes. She knew she was being paid to stay until midnight. Some of the other stalls had already shuttered their windows for the night. They were probably the owners of the kiosks. A hired worker wouldn't be able to make that call, no matter how useless it was to stand here waiting in the cold for a customer.

She stamped her feet again and turned her thoughts back to Theo and little Geoff. They'd both been so good this year—especially with their father leaving. They deserved the best Christmas ever. And if Pomme had anything to say about it, between working the crêpe stand, cleaning offices until well past midnight and selling hot wine until her fingers froze—she was going to make sure they got it.

She stared down at the line of kiosks and booths, their lights blinking off one by one down the Champs-Élysées. She knew the ones closer to the Arc de Triomphe had gotten the most crowds. It wasn't as busy where Omar's booth was, so much further down the famous boulevard, but she'd still gotten plenty of pedestrian traffic. She glanced at the cash box. Omar had told her to bring it with her to the OmniManger office in the morning. Guy—Omar's second in command—had suggested leaving it in the booth overnight, saying the gendarmes would watch the booths. But he'd only suggested that because he didn't trust her not to steal from the box if she brought it home overnight.

She glanced at her watch. This was ridiculous. She hadn't had a customer in forty-five minutes. It was too cold and too late for anyone to be promenading out and about looking for a hot drink. If she closed up fifteen minutes early—who was to know?—she would have time to go home and check on the boys before rushing off to her office cleaning job. She drummed her gloved fingers on the counter and tried to decide if she dared close up when her eye caught the form of someone approaching.

Oh well, she thought, putting the smile on her face that Monsieur Omar insisted all the tourists required and that all his employees must provide. She glanced at the space heater she had been about to turn off. There wasn't enough wine in the pot to make even two cups, but Omar wouldn't be happy if she added another bottle this late in the night. Maybe the customer didn't want wine? She looked up as the figure approached and felt her throat close. It wasn't a tourist.

She clutched the rim of the counter and forced herself to breathe normally. He walked to the front of the counter and shot his arm out at her.

At the end of the arm was the ugly profile of a black snub-nosed pistol pointed at her chest.

6

A s I walked, I found myself warming up. The activity also helped to soften my disappointment a bit at Jean-Marc not showing. It had been too much to hope for. I didn't think he did it on purpose—stand me up—that wasn't Jean-Marc's style. I think he genuinely wanted to see me. And then realized he wasn't ready.

The snow had started back up, but I wasn't worried. It was still falling only lightly and was actually quite magical. I wouldn't be too covered by the time I got home and how often does one get to walk home in the snow in Paris?

The lights in the near distance glowed festively as if they were lighting my way home. I knew I was seeing the glow from the Christmas market booths that lined the Champs-Élysées. The *Marchés de Noël* are a long tradition in France, dating back to the Middle Ages. They sell everything from handmade tree decorations and wooden gifts to hot mulled wine and Eiffel Tower cookies. Traditionally held in the town square, these festive little chalets and kiosks really add a bright spot to the short winter days that usher in the Advent season.

I'd already taken Robbie to a few of them at least a half a dozen times—they are literally all over Paris—for cookies and cocoa. I'm sorry the States don't have them because I've decided that nothing says *Christmas* like a market booth festooned out with tinsel and foiled streamers and shiny ornaments—and of course serving hot mulled wine.

The line of booths was a bit out of the way, but I decided I needed my spirits boosted and the glitter and festivity of the booths were just the ticket. The closer I got, I realized that many of the booths had already closed for the night.

From where I stood, I could see straight down the Champs-Élysées. Nothing and nobody was moving. I sighed. Maybe this was not going to be such a spirit-lifter after all.

Just as I was planning on veering off onto rue Beaujon which would take me home a little quicker, I noticed that there was one booth still serving customers. The thought of a hot wine for the walk home suddenly sounded like exactly what I needed.

I headed for the booth which was surrounded by a long line of now shuttered booths. As I approached, I found myself slowing my pace.

Something wasn't right.

A man was standing at the counter and he was pointing at the girl behind the counter which seemed an odd thing for a customer to be doing. Then I got close enough to see that he wasn't pointing at her at all.

He was aiming at her.

It didn't take Hercules Poirot to see that I was looking at a holdup. I quickly fumbled in my coat pocket for my phone. I ripped off my gloves, dropping them on the ground and snapped a photo of the man in profile as he threatened the cowering woman.

"I can't get into the register," the woman said, her voice high and fearful

"I don't want money!" the man snarled, his voice carrying in the empty night. "You know what I want!"

"No, I don't know," the woman whimpered.

"You think this is a joke?" he shouted, waving the gun closer at her face.

I took in a steadying breath for bravery.

"Excuse me!" I said loudly as I walked up to them.

The man whirled around, pointing the gun at me now, his eyes wild and agitated.

"You should be ashamed of yourself," I said, hoping I sounded calmer than I felt. "Robbing a Christmas market booth!"

"Mind your own business!" he shouted before turning back to the woman in the kiosk.

He clearly wasn't in a mind to listen to me and there was no way I could physically stop him. I dialed the police. But before I could be connected, the woman behind the counter took matters into her own hands. I saw the arc of hot wine as it flew into the gunman's face. He howled and took a step backward.

"*Salope!*" he screamed. "I'll kill you for that!"

The sound of the gunshot reverberated up and down the avenue, shaking the branches of the elm trees around us. I gasped and clutched my phone to my chest.

Dear heavens! Has he shot her?

I held my breath as I watched him race around the side of the kiosk and then disappear into the bushes behind. Confused, I hurried over to the kiosk and leaned over the counter, fully expecting to find the crumpled body of the girl and praying there would be something I could do to help her.

But the kiosk was empty.

7

I looked around the inside of the kiosk in bewilderment but it was clear that the woman had thrown the wine in her assailant's face so she could escape. She didn't have much of a lead on him however. And he had a gun. I finished my call to the police, giving them my location, when I heard the second gun shot.

Chills ran through me as I turned and plunged into the bushes behind the kiosk where I'd seen the gunman go. There were no more gunshots and I tried to determine what that might mean. Had he killed her with the first shot?

The bushes behind all the Christmas market kiosks fronted a wide berm of green hedges that separated the market booths from a residential street of apartment buildings interspersed with retail shops. Naturally, everything was closed at this time of the night. I looked down the berm and noticed a sight that I recognized. When it wasn't Christmas time, this was a well-populated trail leading to a city park that abutted the Champs-Élysées—one that Robbie and I had been to many times.

Had the woman run into the park?

were streetlamps along the path at least so visi-
decent. Unfortunately, it was also decent enough
that the gun man could easily have seen her as she ran. And
likely been able to line up a fairly accurate shot.

I strained to hear, thinking that I should be hearing the
sounds of people running, but I heard nothing. I hurried
down the uneven path of cobble stones and grassy patches. I
tried to remember where the gunshot had come from.

It felt like it had come from the little pocket park straight
ahead, so I kept walking toward it, but more slowly now. The
police were on their way and this was definitely a task for
them, not me. I didn't need to get caught in the crossfire of
whatever robbery-gone-wrong was playing out.

These thoughts—combined with my sworn promise to
Geneviève that I wouldn't do anything dangerous, especially
during the holidays—came to me at the very moment that I
saw on the ground twenty yards in front of me the
unmoving body.

8

The rest of that night went by in a blur of police interrogation, flashing emergency and police vehicular lights and several finger-numbing texts to Geneviève to ask her to stay with the kids until I could get home. I waited for the police by the body of the man I'd discovered. I saw his gun on the ground by his head and was careful not to touch it. I tried to imagine how a man with a gun who was chasing a woman could end up dead himself of an obvious gunshot wound but nothing made sense to me about the picture I was seeing.

When the police came, they took my initial statement along with my overcoat to be examined for gunshot residue. I was then driven to my apartment with the requirement that I come to police headquarters the next morning on the Île de la Cité to give a more detailed statement.

The next morning, I was up early. Geneviève had gone downstairs to her apartment when I came home last night but she was back early this morning putting coffee on while I got ready to leave.

Île de la Cité, where the Paris police headquarters was

located, was a short Metro ride from my apartment. I'd been here many times in my short time living in Paris. Most of those times were for very unhappy reasons.

I waited in a waiting room for someone to come and take my statement. I listened to the phones ringing, the electronic doors clicking open and shut, and the constant murmur of dispatchers speaking into their headsets. There's something inherently nerve-wracking about a police station, I have to say. I used covert breathing techniques to try to stay calm and centered.

I'd worked with the detective in charge of this case before. Or as I'm sure Detective Monique Semple would have phrased it: I'd gotten in the way of her investigation before. I found her just as cold and unpleasant two weeks before Christmas as I ever had.

Fortunately, our time together was brief. As soon as she saw me, she handed me off to a subordinate. I guess she was too important to take witness statements herself, although it was always my understanding that that was the main part of her job. Her sergeant led me to a small windowless room and handed me a pad and pen.

This was the first time I'd been back to the police station since Jean-Marc had retired from the force. I half expected to see people giving me dirty looks about that since I, at least, had no doubt I was one hundred percent to blame. But nobody looked at me or gave me a second look.

I wrote out my statement outlining that I'd come upon what looked like a robbery in progress, whereupon I yelled at the would-be robber, and then saw the woman behind the counter distract him before running away. He fired the gun and then ran after her. I heard another gunshot. And then found his body. And yes, it was the same man who'd threatened the woman.

After I was dismissed, I wandered down the hall toward the exit until I suddenly spotted someone I knew sitting on one of the hall's wooden benches writing on an electronic tablet. Normally due to my face blindness, I'd never have recognized him but he was wearing a name badge on his jacket. David Fontaine was a public defender whom I'd heard nothing but good things about. I'd actually talked with him a few times in passing.

On impulse, I approached him.

"Monsieur Fontaine?"

He looked up. He had dark brown hair and even darker eyes, fringed with thick lashes. A handsome man by any standards.

"Madame Baskerville," he said pleasantly.

I have to say I've always hated my last name—or rather my late husband's last name—but it does sound better in the mouth of a French person.

"I was just wondering if by chance you knew anything about the murder at the Christmas Market last night?"

"I better," he said with a grin. "I'm representing their only suspect."

Without asking, I sat down next to him.

"Who did they arrest?" I prayed he wouldn't tell me it was the poor woman who I'd last seen running for her life.

His sympathetic grimace told me that that was exactly who they'd arrested.

"Her name is Pomme Toussaint," he said. "The police were able to identify her through the owner of the kiosk—a Mo Allard. They picked her up at her apartment."

"They think she killed him?" I asked, truly surprised. "How is that possible? The victim was chasing her with a gun—and shooting!"

"That's not how the police see it, I'm afraid."

"They think she shot *him*? Even though he was the one with the gun?"

"Evidently. Her prints were found on the gun."

I literally could not imagine how that could have happened. The last time I saw the girl—who I guess was more of a grown woman than a girl—she was being chased by the victim. The cops thought that within seconds, she'd somehow gotten a hold of his gun and shot him? It seemed not only impossible but absurd.

"What does she say happened?" I asked.

"I haven't been able to talk to her at length, but suffice to say, she said she didn't do it. She has two little boys who went into care last night. It's all pretty sad. It's the main reason I took the case."

"Who's the gunman?"

"They're referring to him as *the victim*," he said with a snort. "His name is Guy Monet. I don't know anything else about him yet."

I sighed and felt a light veil of sadness drift over me.

"I just wish I knew why self-defense isn't a factor here," I said.

"I honestly don't know."

The whole situation was particularly frustrating especially because I no longer had a man on the inside—Jean-Marc—who might be able to tell me *why* the cops thought Madame Toussaint killed her assailant. And how.

All I knew was that it didn't feel right

On top of the seeming impossibility of it all, I couldn't imagine how this poor woman must feel knowing her children would be in state foster care over Christmas while their mother was in jail.

Especially if she's innocent.

9

A fter I left for the police station, I hit my favorite *boulangerie* on the way home. I typically went there after walking Robbie to school, but he was on school break now. I popped in to pick up a croissant and latté for Geneviève as a thank-you for watching the kids for me this morning.

As I made my way down rue de Laborde to my apartment, I worked hard to put the whole sad situation of Pomme Toussaint and her children out of my mind. This morning before I'd left for the police station, Robbie had been whatever the French word for *bonkers* is when he'd awakened to snow. He's normally a sweet little fellow and very compliant, thank goodness. But I knew it was going to be all Geneviève could do to keep him occupied while I was gone.

As soon as I got back to the apartment, I put together a couple of sandwiches, Maddie's formula bottles, and a thermos of tomato soup and bundled both Robbie and Maddie up for an outing. Frankly, I'd have liked nothing better than to enjoy a nap when I got home, but it was not to be. The recent cold weather meant that Izzy, my sweet little French bulldog, had not been getting the exercise she needed so she would need to come too. I added the looped handle of her leash to the handlebar on Maddie's stroller and made my way down the tiny elevator of my apartment building.

Once outside, we headed east toward Parc Monceau although that was not our destination today. I needed to pick up a few things from the shops. The streets would be decorated for the Christmas season which I knew Robbie would love. Sure enough, as soon as we turned off our residential street of rue de Laborde onto boulevard Malesherbes, the streetlamps were festooned with dancing gingerbread men and candy canes. I made a mental note to take Robbie to the *Galeries Lafayette* sometime before Christmas. The storefront windows were a wonderland of the season, complete with a working ice-skating rink with colorful little skating bears wearing bowties made of glitter and capped with little green wreaths peppered with holly.

I never got tired of seeing the smiles from people we passed, all of them assuming I was the doting grandmother of these two and they'd be partially right about that. Robbie was the surprise lovechild of my cheating and now deceased husband and his secretary—who was unfortunately also deceased. Although Robbie is no blood relation to me, I'm not giving him up until I pack him off to college and there's a good chance not even then.

Maddie on the other hand is my blood-related granddaughter but her story is only a little less outlandish than Robbie's. She is the result of a stolen egg of my daughter's that was then inseminated and implanted into a surrogate who died giving birth to her.

Correction. Nahla did not die as a result of giving birth

to Maddie. She died of a bullet to the chest. But enough of that.

Maddie was "a good baby," as the saying goes. She was very smiley and almost never fussed. Her mother hadn't been like that when she was little and I wondered for a moment if Maddie took after her father. Just thinking of Abd-El-Kader, the scoundrel who had fertilized Catherine's stolen eggs, made me want to hit something. But then again, Maddie was a prize beyond measure and, if not for the crime committed by Abd-El-Kader in Dubai, I wouldn't have her.

It's so strange how life is sometimes, isn't it?

The first shop we went into was a chocolate shop, always dangerous to visit with a small child. Robbie was normally well-behaved but this shop even tempted *me* to dive face first into their towering truffles display. They did a passion fruit yule log that I dream of for months after Christmas. I gave Robbie his own gingerbread man to chew on while I made my selections: almond and orange scones, a chocolate Christmas ball studded with nuts and berries and wrapped in a shiny ganache glaze, and a dozen citrus gingerbread men that I've been wanting to try ever since Thanksgiving.

Once back out on the street, I turned in the direction of the neighborhood Monoprix. Because it would just be me and the children with Geneviève this year for Christmas Day dinner, there wasn't a whole lot to buy and virtually nothing that needed advanced ordering.

As we headed down rue Balzac towards the mega shopping store, which is like a French Target only smaller and includes a top-ranked bakery and over one hundred kinds of yoghurt, my mind drifted back to the unfortunate matter of Pomme Toussaint. I couldn't begin to imagine how brokenhearted she must feel right now.

I wondered where her husband was. David said he wasn't in the picture anymore, but I didn't know if that meant not with the kids either? Additionally, David seemed totally happy to share what he knew with me about the case.

He'd told me the victim's name was Guy Monet and just as soon as I had a few minutes to myself I intended to dig around on the Internet to find out who he was, if he had a record, and why he had come after Pomme Toussaint with a gun. I remember him shouting, *"I don't want the stupid cash register money!"* Which is not the sort of thing most thieves say in the middle of an armed robbery.

So if it wasn't money, why was he there?

10

A fter returning home with my bag of goodies, I managed to get Robbie down for a nap—mostly with threats about what Santa would and wouldn't be looking for in a "good boy." I put Maddie in her baby bouncer in the kitchen while I prepped the chicken I'd picked up for tonight's dinner.

Geneviève would be over this evening to help with the Christmas tree and general memory-making stuff for the holidays—mostly for Robbie but I'd enjoy it all too. I have to say I found myself thinking about Jean-Marc more and more during this time of year. We'd been together on and off for four years, but we'd always managed to be together during the holidays. I thought about that text message he'd sent me—the one he'd clearly thought better of. And I wished we could have met at least to start mending fences.

But I understood why he might not want to.

Although David was awfully nice, even if he was at least ten years too young for me, I knew I wasn't ready for something new.

When my phone rang, I wasn't even surprised to see it

was David. I took my coffee and sat down in the dining room, with Maddie—who'd conveniently fallen asleep by now—still in her bouncer.

"Hey," I said. "This is a nice surprise."

"Well, I did promise I'd tell you anything I found out," David said. "I think you're going to want to hear this."

"I'm all ears."

"It turns out Pomme knew the gun man. They both worked for the same firm."

"Interesting. So why did he pull a gun on her?"

"The police said it was because she'd accused him of sexual assault through their company."

"Okay, so I guess he was trying to get her to recant the charge? But why do the cops think she killed him? He approached *her* in the kiosk!"

"They're saying Pomme must have had a gun with her, making the killing premeditated. They're trying to find evidence that she actually lured him to the kiosk."

"Wait. There are two guns?"

"Yes, the one that Guy threatened her with, that's the one that was found at the scene with her prints on."

"But that's not the one that killed him?"

"Apparently not. The police think Pomme tossed the murder weapon in the Seine on her way home that night."

"Or there's another gunman! Someone who shot Guy and took off with the gun!"

"Pomme said she didn't see anyone else."

"But if Pomme had a gun, why would she pick up Guy's gun after she'd shot him?"

"I agree, it's a puzzle."

"And if Guy went to the kiosk to demand she retract her complaint against him, then why did I hear him shouting about money?"

"Because, regardless of what the police say is Pomme's motive for killing him, I don't think he was there about the sexual assault. There *was* a money issue that was much more important to him."

"You've uncovered something?"

"Their boss was a man named Omar Blanchet. Guy was his second-in-command and I guess Omar treated Guy like the son he never had. The partner, Mo Allard, said it was common knowledge that Omar planned to settle everything on Guy in his will."

"Is that even legal? I thought by French law it could only be the man's children who inherited."

"With the right lawyer, you can get around the law."

"Did Omar have any biological children?"

"He did. A daughter."

"Presumably she intended to sue to overturn the will."

"Presumably."

I struggled to put all the pieces together.

"I assume Omar has recently shuffled off the mortal coil?"

"Tuesday night. The same night as the attack."

The realization of what must have happened bloomed in my brain like a flower.

"Why did Guy think Pomme knew anything about the money?"

"Because he'd recently been told—on Omar's death bed—that he'd left the money to her instead."

I whistled. "So, Guy attacked Pomme because he found out that Omar left his money to her instead?"

"He did," David said with a sigh. "Except it turned out that Omar *didn't* leave his money to Pomme. The will hadn't been read yet at the time that Guy came after Pomme at the Christmas market kiosk. When it was read—this morning, actually—it turned out that the money *was* left to Guy in the will as promised."

"Why did Guy—?"

"Are you asking why Omar told him he was giving the money to Pomme? It seems Omar was an irascible bastard who enjoyed torturing people. From what I can gather, he told Guy that to rattle his cage."

"Consider it rattled," Claire said, shaking her head. "Guy died because of a lie."

"Well, he really died because he reacted badly to a lie," David pointed out.

"I guess this means the daughter gets the inheritance free and clear. What do you know about her?"

"All I know right now is that her name is Cherise Blanchet."

"Got an address for her?"

———

11

That night, Geneviève and I did a stupendous job of recreating Christmas bliss for the kids. My apartment is seven hundred square feet with two bedrooms and a kitchen the size of my butler's pantry back in Atlanta. The whole place is tiny by American standards. I'm surprised how quickly I'd gotten used to its pared-down size. In order to fit a small Christmas tree in the corner of my living room, I'd put one of my occasional chairs in my bedroom—not that there was room for it in there.

That and some fragrant swags of fir boughs and white candles on the mantle of my fireplace completed my Christmas décor. I added some fragrant candles—fir and cinnamon scents—and set a large bowl of gold ornaments on one of the side tables.

I clearly remember how Catherine was at Christmastime and I definitely took a moment to enjoy Robbie's pleasure in it. At four, he was at the perfect age. He knew what it was all about now—about Baby Jesus and presents—and he knew he had to wait for both, which of course just intensified the pleasure.

The only thing that really bothered me—and Geneviève made sure I never forgot it for a moment—was the fact that Catherine was still largely incommunicado with me. My unease and worry were further intensified by the fact that, except for Maddie's big brown eyes, dark hair and olive skin, I was living with this adorable creature who was the very picture of Catherine as a baby. And Catherine had no idea she existed.

After a quiet evening of television and puzzles, Robbie went to bed early and Maddie was, thank goodness, already sleeping through the night. My teenage sitter Haley usually helped me with both Robbie and Maddie but her ski trip was still another six days.

Not that I'm counting the days.

The next morning, largely on the pretext of buying Geneviève's Christmas present, I slipped away while she watched Izzy and the children. David had texted me Cherise Blanchet's address and I was hoping to have a word with her. I was very aware that Cherise had just lost her father—Omar—but since I also knew that she wasn't mentioned in his will, I didn't expect to find her ripping her hair out with grief. And I didn't.

Cherise lived in Le Marais which has a good mix of wealthy upscale apartments and some faintly slummy ones. Her apartment building was one of the former.

She met me at the door with a tiny Yorkshire terrier in her arms. I like dog people and I always tend to give them the benefit of the doubt. Within reason, of course.

"Madame Blanchet?" I said as we shook hands. "Thank you for seeing me."

When setting up the appointment with her on the

phone that morning I'd told her I was working with the Paris police on Guy Monet's murder. She never asked me in what capacity so I didn't offer any details.

She led me into her apartment where a tiny and very tasteful Christmas tree sat in the corner on a table. We sat across from each other on facing couches in the salon.

"What I can do to help?" she asked mechanically.

She had a thin, sharp-boned face with narrow lips and shrewd eyes. She wore her limp dishwater blonde hair to her shoulders with no particular effort made to style it.

"I wanted to ask you if you were concerned about your father's relationship with Guy Monet," I said.

As far as the interview was concerned, I'd decided that I needed to come out with guns blazing. In my experience it was the best way to catch people off guard—and possibly startle them into blurting out the truth.

"Not for a minute," she said with a snort. "French law dictates that my father's money would come to me."

I didn't ask her if she'd planned to sue if Guy hadn't died because there seemed no point. Her manner was completely confident that, dead or alive, Guy was not getting her inheritance.

"Did you know Guy Monet well?"

"I just knew him from my father's business."

"Do you do anything for your father's business?"

"I didn't before, but I intend to now. I have some ideas I want to implement."

"So, you own an equal share in the business with Mo Allard?"

"That's right."

I didn't say anything, but I wondered how Mo felt about Cherise jumping in with her "ideas" about how to run his business.

"Did you hear the rumor that the reason Guy was at the Christmas Market booth was because he thought he had been left out of the will?" I asked.

"It wasn't a rumor. My father told him on his death bed that he was out. I know because I was there."

"But your father never changed his will."

"He was just making Guy squirm. My father wasn't a nice man. I don't know anyone who liked him besides Guy and Robert."

"Robert?"

"Robert Granger, my father's personal assistant. He did everything but tie my father's shoelaces for him and probably licked his boots too."

"He must be upset about your father's passing."

"I imagine."

"Was he also close to Guy Monet?"

Cherise frowned as if trying to think about it.

"I guess so. They hung out a lot together. Now that you mention it, Robert losing both of them—my father and Guy —that's quite a one-two punch. I hadn't thought about that until now. I should say something to him, I guess."

"Do you know him very well?"

"Not at all. I'd heard through the office gossip mill that he was having a little financial trouble but my father paid him well. It was his own fault, if he was."

I couldn't help but think how heartless Cherise sounded. Clearly Robert had suffered a terrible loss. In fact, much more than she had. And yet she was walking away with all the money.

"Well, thank you, Madame Blanchet," I said, standing up. "I appreciate you seeing me, especially during this sad time."

She set the little dog down on the carpet and he immediately wet the rug. Cherise watched him but didn't seem perturbed.

"You should ask Pomme about Robert," she said.

I was taken aback since I assumed that if Cherise didn't really know Robert who worked in the office, she'd hardly know the crêpe girl who was never in the office.

"Pomme knew Robert?" I asked.

"I'd say so," she said as she reached into her pocket for a tissue that she then used to blot up the stain on the carpet. "She was his girlfriend."

12

I have to say, the French really get into ice-skating at Christmas.

Most parks during this time of year are set up with ice rinks. The Tuileries is turned into a virtual replica of the rink at Rockefeller Center, but my favorite rink is surrounded by a forest of twinkling Christmas trees on La Cour Jardin at the legendary Hôtel Plaza Athénée.

For more than a century, this hotel has been a chic fixture on Avenue de Montaigne. It's considered a *grand palais* hotel any time of year. But at Christmas, it turns into a breathtaking wonderland that would have Scrooge squealing in delight.

When I left Cherise's and texted David, who suggested we meet there for a drink to confer on our notes, I was only too happy to do so.

I must have been closer to the hotel than David because I got there first. The extraordinary thing about this partic- ular hotel—besides its amazing history from Dietrich to Chanel—is that it has no fewer than six bars in it. I think that's because the French believe that there's a certain feeling unique to each experience. One of them is known for its grand Royal Table crafted from antique Breccia marble and its walls of twenty thousand gold leaves beneath a gilded ceiling.

The bar where David and I had agreed to meet was called sensibly enough *Le Bar* and even without the gold leaves and ceiling, it was still elegant. The decorations were the epitome of seasonal display, with multicolored fairy lights strung in the branches of the silver maples—potted and very real—and hanging ornaments from the chandeliers that were nothing short of breathtaking.

I ordered a Kir Royale—for the holiday color if nothing else—and waited for David to arrive. The thing I've learned about Paris after living here for four years is that clothes matter and they especially matter during the holidays. I've gotten in the habit of dressing up when I go out. Today, I was happy for that habit. I wore a vintage Saint Laurent dress with tights and Stuart Weitzman boots, a Tory Burch coat that was more streamlined than it was bulky but still kept me warm, and my favorite Stella McCartney shoulder bag that I'd found for only four hundred euros at a favorite vintage shop.

When David arrived, his cheeks pink from hurrying and his brown hair wind-blown, I was struck by how handsome he was. With my face blindness, whenever I see someone after any kind of absence, it's always like meeting them for the first time. And first-time meetings are always rather magical.

He kissed me on both cheeks and then sat next to me at the bar.

"This was a great idea," I said, waving to the bar. I still wasn't sure whether he was coming on to me or if this was just how he did business.

"It's especially nice at Christmas, don't you think?"

He unwound his scarf from around his neck and dropped it on the chair beside him. I tried to remember if I'd ever even seen an American man wear a neck scarf. As soon as he was served his drink, I dove right in.

"Did you know that Pomme was dating someone from the office?" I asked.

David frowned. "She was?"

"Shouldn't Pomme have told you?" I asked with an arched eyebrow.

He sighed.

"She's very close lipped," he said. "Frankly, there's more tears than words when we meet."

"How horrible all this must be for her."

"It's going to be even more horrible if she doesn't start talking to me."

"Is there any chance *I* could talk to her?"

"I can arrange that. Thanks, Claire. I think that would help a lot."

I beamed at how eager he seemed to be for my help—again, not something I was used to in these kinds of investigations.

"At this point," David said, sipping his drink, "I'm just trying to find anybody who might be a better suspect than Pomme. But it's pretty hard to work around those finger-prints on the gun."

"Except it wasn't the murder weapon."

"No, and trust me, that's helpful but it doesn't clear her. Not by a long shot."

"The guy she's supposed to be seeing in the office is Omar Blanchet's personal assistant, Robert Granger," I said. "I was thinking I might track him down. Any problem with me doing that?"

"None at all. I feel guilty making you do all my legwork."

"Well, don't. I'm happy to help. Do you have any news?"

David ran his hand through his hair, and I could smell the cold air coming off him in faint whiffs.

"The cops did a search of Guy's apartment this morning," he said. "They discovered a treasure trove of emails and other documents on his computer that might help us."

"In what way?"

"Well, there was an exchange of angry emails between him and Liesel Blanchet, Omar's widow. She came right out and threatened to have the will overturned if Omar insisted on naming him in his will."

"Wow. How did it benefit her to tell Guy that?"

"Your guess is as good as mine." He grinned. "And you are more than welcome to ask her yourself." He reached over and took my hand.

"Meanwhile," he said, "I'm going to get an interview time set up for you to see Pomme." He looked into my eyes, his hand still on mind. "I can't tell you how glad I am to be working with you on this, Claire. Seriously."

13

The next morning, as I was sitting in the waiting room at the Paris police department on the Île de la Cité, waiting to be allowed to visit Pomme Toussaint, I put a call in to Mo Allard, Omar's partner at Omni-Manger. I spoke with his secretary who told me in no uncertain terms that Monsieur Allard was not available and to kindly direct all my questions to the company press secretary. She hung up before she could tell me who that was.

When they finally ushered me into the room where I could talk with Pomme—through a glass with phone handsets on each side—I was a bit shocked to see how disheveled she looked from the young woman I'd seen manning the hot wine booth two nights ago.

The two nights in jail aside, I could see Pomme had had a hard life as she was forced to raise her two boys alone on one paycheck. I knew the basics of her curriculum vitae: after her husband left her, she'd worked for Omar Blanchet for two years, making crêpes in the Latin quarter, cleaning offices in the area, and doing seasonal work in the Christmas booth on the Champs-Élysées.

"Hello, Madame Toussaint," I said. "My name is Claire Baskerville. I'm working with your lawyer to help you."

She nodded as if to confirm that David had said I'd be coming today. I'd debated most of the morning over my opening for this interview and finally settled on the direct approach. First, I had no idea if the police would allow us the full thirty minutes—they often didn't. Second, I didn't want Pomme to see me as smarmy or officious. I wanted her to hear my sincerity and for me, the best way to do that was not to beat around the bush.

"I was there that night," I said. "The night Guy Monet was killed."

Her eyes widened but I couldn't detect guilt or guile in them.

"You wanted mulled wine?" she asked sarcastically.

"I was thinking about it. Then I saw this guy holding you at gunpoint."

She shook her head.

"He must have been out of his head," she said. "I still can't believe he's dead."

"And you have no idea who might have shot him?"

"Don't you think I would've said if I did?"

"Probably. Unless you're trying to protect someone."

"Madame Baskerville, I have two little boys who need me at home. I am not so noble that I would take the blame if I could help it."

Now was the moment when things might get a bit unpleasant, I thought, but I reminded myself that if my being tough with her now resulted in her release down the road, it would be worth it.

"I don't think your lawyer knew you had a boyfriend at the office," I said.

I wasn't directly suggesting that she might be trying to

protect Robert, but I'd already registered that it was a possibility. Even loving mothers can be blinded by passion if the hook was set deep enough.

Pomme frowned as if she wasn't sure who I was talking about.

"Robert Granger?" I prompted.

She rolled her eyes.

"We hooked up one time but only because I was lonely and had had too much to drink."

"Cherise Blanchet seems to think it was more than that."

"I have no idea who Cherise Blanchet is."

"Omar Blanchet's daughter?"

She shrugged. "I didn't even know Monsieur Omar had a daughter."

Was any of this believable?

"Did you come into the office much?"

"Almost never."

"So how did you meet Robert?"

She snorted. "At a company Christmas party last year." As soon as she said it, her eyes filled with tears as if realizing how different Christmas was going to be this year. I was tempted to ask if her husband was still living at home last year but decided it wasn't relevant.

"When did Guy Monet sexually assault you?"

Pomme made a face and began to pick at the hem of her prison tunic.

"Two months ago," she said.

"Where?"

This was key since Pomme had already made a point of saying she was rarely in the office.

"I clean offices at night," she said angrily. "And one of them is down the hall from OmniManger. Guy must have seen me go in because as soon as I started mopping the floor, he came up behind me."

"You didn't lock the door after you went in?"

"No. I guess I should have," she said, giving me a flat look with her eyes narrowed.

"And he raped you?"

She looked away.

"I fought him off. But it was still horrible."

She looked up, her face closed. She crossed her arms across her chest.

"I didn't make the complaint against him to have him thrown in jail. I just wanted him to take responsibility for it."

"And maybe lose his job?"

"If that's what happened, so be it," she said, stonily.

"When did you file the complaint?"

"Last week."

"Why did you wait so long?"

"I don't know. I just did."

I gave her a moment and let the silence build. I find this very effective in unnerving suspects and while I dearly hoped that Pomme was not the person who killed Guy, still, I could tell she wasn't being forthcoming with me.

"Had you heard that Omar Blanchet told Guy he'd named you as his beneficiary instead of him?"

"No. And the very idea is ludicrous."

"Why?"

"I've spoken to Monsieur Omar maybe two times. He didn't know me from his Ficus plant."

I definitely picked up that she was bitter but also afraid, and the dark circles under her eyes told me she was working too hard and was battling exhaustion. And now, she had the horror of worrying about her little boys too.

"The police found your prints on Guy Monet's gun," I said.

"I know. I'm an idiot. When I realized he wasn't chasing me anymore, I doubled back and saw him on the ground. I went to him because I thought he might have tripped, and maybe the gun went off and shot him in the leg or something."

"So, you picked up his gun?"

She groaned. "Yes, as I said, I am an idiot. I can only say that a part of me thought to take it so he couldn't use it on me. As soon as I realized he was way past that, I dropped it and ran."

The uniformed police guard opened the door behind Pomme and instructed her to stand up.

The visit was over. She glanced briefly at me before hanging up and blurted out, "You are a mother?"

I nodded, already feeling the lump form in my throat.

"I'm innocent of this," she said as the guard put his hand on her shoulder. "Please, help me get back home to my boys."

14

I'm not exactly sure what I'd learned from my fifteen minutes with Pomme, but I nonetheless sat in the waiting room to jot down the basics so that, when I spoke with David later tonight, I'd have the facts straight. Then, I put another call in to Mo Allard and was again told that Monsieur Allard was not available.

How does the woman answering the phone know I'm not a potential client? I thought with annoyance as I gathered my things and stepped out into the cold gray late morning of a perfect Paris day.

I often walk to help me get my thoughts in order, which is why I rarely take the Metro unless I'm late. Today I knew that Geneviève was fine until lunchtime. That gave me a solid two hours to think and walk. It occurred to me that Omar Blanchet's home address could be considered somewhat on the way home to my own apartment, so I headed that way.

With the possible exception of being able to talk to his widow Liesel Blanchet, I didn't have a whole lot of expectations beyond getting a better idea of who the man had been.

When I arrived at the apartment building on rue Royale in the eighth arrondissement, I was not at all surprised to see how upscale and well-to-do it was.

On a classic Haussmann street with uniform apartment buildings featuring creamy façades, black wrought-iron Juliette balconies, and mansard roofs, Cherise's apartment was like something out of the movie *Ratatouille*. Each of the streetlamps on this avenue had an elegant spiral of white lights that, even in the morning shone bright. A bench was nearby, and as I'd walked a long way from the Île de la Cité, I sat down to rest my feet and enjoy the pretty street with its understated but enchanting Christmas decorations.

As I sat there staring up at the building, I tried to imagine what Pomme must think of how her employer lived while she cleaned offices and worked late nights flipping crêpes to make ends meet for her little boys. She struck me as a hard woman, yes, but one who'd been *made* hard by her circumstances.

"You looking to buy an apartment?"

I turned around to see a very old woman standing beside the bench, leaning on a cane. She was well dressed and her eyes were sharp. I was astonished that she'd been able to sneak up on me.

I must be more tired than I thought.

"No," I said. "Just admiring how beautiful it is."

"You are English?" she said, hobbling closer.

"American."

She nodded and sat down.

"I thought you might be one of the mourners," she said. "They've been coming all morning to pay their respects."

Of course! With Omar's recent passing, there would be a showing of the body at his residence.

"I didn't know him," I admitted.

"But you know of him," she said.

I turned to give her my full attention. In my experience, nosy neighbors were the gold standard of casual witnesses. Especially the older ones. They were usually bored enough to take particular notice of their surroundings and the people who populated them.

"Are you a neighbor of Monsieur Blanchet's?" I asked.

She snorted. "I have lived in this building for forty years. Long before Monsieur Blanchet."

"Did he raise his family here?"

Her eyes narrowed as she regarded me.

"You mean his daughter and his first wife?"

I hadn't known that Liesel *wasn't* Cherise's mother. But hearing it now, it didn't surprise me.

"Yes," she said. "They all lived here as happy as clams. Rotten clams!" She smacked the ground with the tip of her cane. "He threw them both out. I heard *she* died but the girl is still in Paris."

I turned to look at the house.

"It's a sad business," I said, not sure what else there was to say.

"All starting with that boy," she said.

I turned to look at her, my ears sharp. "What boy?"

"The one he had with some whore," she said, her lip curled in disgust. "He threw them out too until it looked like he wasn't going to get a son any other way. Named him after a painter. I told my husband that Omar Blanchet was delusional. And my husband, God rest his soul, always said he had the money to do it."

But I'd stopped listening.

Omar Blanchet had an unrecognized biological son he named after a painter?

Seriously?

I stood up, reaching for my phone as I did. I rushed off, throwing my thanks over my shoulder as I called up David's number. The old neighbor told me how rude I was and how she hadn't expected much more from an American.

But I barely heard her.

I was pretty sure I'd just discovered that Guy Monet was Omar's biological son.

15

That afternoon I relieved Geneviève, who went home to take a well-earned nap, and after getting a quick debrief over the phone with David, I was determined to do Christmassy stuff with Robbie.

It was important to me that I didn't get so focused on Pomme's case that I forgot the holiday for my own two little ones. Granted, them missing out on the magic of Christmas for one year that neither of them would remember in ten years' time wasn't as important as doing everything I could to bring Pomme home to her children.

Honestly, I supposed I was doing it more for me than anyone else. With Catherine and Jean-Marc both so far away—emotionally as well as physically—I really needed to lean on the rituals and traditions of the season to remind myself of something fundamental.

In any case, I was sure Pomme and David could handle me taking the afternoon off while I baked cookies with Robbie and played Raffi's Christmas songs on the HomePod.

After rolling out the dough and forcing myself not to help Robbie use the candy cane and wreathe cookie cutouts,

I popped the cookies into the oven and allowed him to mix the confectioner's sugar and milk to make the frosting. My kitchen looked like the set of the Great British Bake-Off had been fire-bombed, with batter and sprinkles visible as far up as the top kitchen cabinets. I even found a silver nonpareil on one of the blades of the overhead fan.

While Robbie created culinary Armageddon in my kitchen Maddie alternately cooed happily with her skunk stuffed animal, napped and waved her little fists in the air. These were the times that it hurt the most to imagine Catherine not knowing her own child. Every day that went by that I didn't tell her made it a thousand times worse—or it would—as soon as she discovered the truth.

My only defense for not telling her was that I really didn't believe Catherine could handle it. When confronted with the shocking fact of the stolen eggs last year, she was initially outraged at the ineptitude of the freezing clinic, but soon became extremely apathetic. It was almost as if she didn't care if the eggs were retrieved. I'm not sure if I'm making that up in my head to justify what I am doing now, or if I'm recalling accurately.

I do know that Catherine had some mental health challenges last year—made worse I'm sure by the experience of being kidnapped during her last visit to me. Dropping in her lap a baby she was never pregnant with, or even telling her about it so she could feel guilty about not being up to the task—well, I can honestly say I felt like I was protecting her until she could handle it better.

Which I knew was going to be no defense at all when the time came to come clean with her.

I glanced at Maddie who had ripped off her sock and flung it across the room, presumably at Izzy who ran over to snatch it up.

Will Catherine ever be able to forgive me for not telling her?

The ding of the oven alarm reminded me that burnt cookies weren't very festive. I pulled them out, warning Robbie not to touch the pan, and set him down at the dining room table with two bowls of sprinkles and the mostly mixed frosting in five separate bowls beside five tiny bottles of food coloring. I only hoped the food coloring was washable since I'd just had the dining chairs reupholstered.

While Robbie happily mixed the most inedible shades of colors for his Christmas cookies, I put another call in to Mo Allard. You know what they say about the definition of insanity? I don't know why I was bothering because Allard's gatekeeper made the Directorate of Military Intelligence and the CIA look like a Mothers Morning Out playgroup. Clearly, I was going to have to do some stalking if I was going to talk to him

After exhausting Robbie with icing cookies and licking bowls, I put Maddie down for a proper nap and parked the young man in front of the television so I could spend an hour on the Internet. I immediately found conclusive proof that Guy Monet was in fact Omar Blanchet's biological son.

Finding people is what I do for a living, so connecting the dots on Guy's paternity when I knew everyone's names was a no-brainer. It occurred to me that if I could figure it out, other people could too.

In my mind, the fact that Guy was Omar's biological child changed a lot because it now made—in a single brush stroke, if you can excuse the painting reference—a lot of people who'd been in the clear before deeply suspect.

It meant that Cherise had a much bigger motive than before—*if she'd known the truth about Guy.* Now there was no hope of breaking the will since he would have absolutely inherited. Her only chance would have been to sue so that she could be awarded at least a share of the money with him.

That is, of course, unless he was dead. As far as I was concerned this definitely pushed Cherise to the top of the suspects list.

It also made Liesel Blanchet a more viable suspect. One child was hard enough to wrest an inheritance from.

Two would have been downright impossible.

16

———————

The next morning, my interim babysitter came over so that I could have the day to finish up a little last-minute Christmas shopping and track down a few more people in the Pomme Toussaint case. I did ask myself whether I was working this case *gratis* because I wanted to help a single mother at Christmastime or because it meant I got to see more of David.

In the end, I decided it didn't matter.

After a rejuvenating hour spent alone at a café with a *noisette* and a croissant, I made my way to the seventh *arrondissment* not far from Les Invalides to where I knew Robert Granger lived. In spite of the colder temperatures, it was a pleasant walk at this time of the morning. I hadn't needed David's help in finding Robert Granger's home address since tracking people is kind of my thing.

I'd debated knocking on his door or lying in wait on the street outside his apartment. When I got to his street, I saw there was a very tidy little pocket park right across from his building.

I went to the park intending that if I didn't find anyone

there who looked like Robert Granger, I would then knock on his door. Paris apartment buildings tended to have rather sophisticated security codes for entry. While I had a few tricks for getting in without knowing the codes, it sometimes took more time than I wanted to spend. Like today, for instance.

If he was in the park, I planned to use the screen shot of Robert Granger from his company's website to identify him. The problem is, my face blindness makes it impossible for me to recognize faces I've seen even moments earlier. Nevertheless, with Robert's photo on my cellphone, I felt confident I'd be able to recognize anyone who matched his appearance.

It was a sweet little park, with lots of green benches and wide pathways through the dormant flowerbeds. There was even a small pond with a little stone bridge arching over it. The park was lovely in December and I could only imagine how pretty it must be in April.

I instantly discounted the three women I saw in the park and the old fellow reading a book on a park bench. He was a curiosity though, since it was a cold and a bench is a hard place to sit for very long. However, he was well-dressed so he could merely be escaping a hectic, noisy holiday household.

A single man with a Jack Russell terrier was walking slowly beside what I was sure would be a luscious flowerbed in the spring. He walked aimlessly without any seeming direction—as we all do when outside in uncomfortable weather for no other reason than to get our dogs to relieve themselves.

I moved toward him to get a look at his face, assuming that if he noticed me, I could always say I mistook him for someone else. He looked at me before I was halfway to him.

Unfortunately, I hadn't studied the cellphone photo well enough to know whether his face and the photo were remotely alike.

Oh well. Time to punt.

"Monsieur Granger?" I called as I caught up with him.

"*Oui?*" he said, frowning. "Do I know you?"

Ignoring his question, I nodded at his dog.

"You have a beautiful Jack Russell. I love that breed. Is she friendly?"

"But of course," he said, his face going suddenly from suspicious to proud.

Dog people have an Achilles heel whenever anyone compliments and praises their precious pet. I'm told cat people are much the same. I petted Robert's dog for a moment, then straightened up to see that Robert seemed much happier to make my acquaintance.

"My name is Claire Baskerville. I'm working with David Fontaine who is defending Pomme Toussaint."

Robert instantly began nodding, his face clear of all reservations.

"Absolutely. Anything I can do to help," he said. "Have you seen Pomme? Is she okay?"

"She's okay," I said as we moved to a nearby bench. "Not great, as you can imagine."

"I cannot believe any of this has happened," he said as he allowed his dog a longer leash to sniff the nearby bushes.

"I'm sure you must be reeling," I said. "First your boss, then Guy. You were close?"

He let out a breath.

"Yes, to both," he said. I saw his eyes glisten as he struggled to hold back tears. "And for this to happen to Pomme is....*incroyable.*"

"I would appreciate all the help you can give me," I said,

ready to launch into my questions but also wanting to be sensitive to the fact that he knew all these people personally. On top of everything, he might be out of a job.

He quickly wiped his eyes. "Yes, of course. Anything."

"Can you tell me why Omar Blanchett might have told Guy that he'd left the money to Pomme instead of him?"

Robert groaned.

"I can't, no. I have a theory though." He sighed heavily again. "Monsieur Blanchet was a very moral, caring man, but also a very complex one. And he could be hard. In many ways he was not unlike my own father who was loving but felt he had a duty to guide me. My dreams were not unimportant to him, but he always urged me to be realistic."

"And Omar was doing that with Guy?" I prompted, wanting him to get back to the point.

"I think so, yes. You know about the assault complaint that Pomme made against Guy?"

I nodded.

"Monsieur Blanchet was very disappointed in Guy over that," he said.

"Do you think Monsieur Blanchet was reprimanding Guy when he told him he wouldn't inherit after all?"

"That's my theory, yes. Especially since Monsieur Blanchet never changed his will. What else could it be? He and Guy were close. I think it was like a loving but disappointed father attempting to correct a beloved but sometimes wayward son. I think Monsieur Blanchet was reminding Guy to mind his manners better."

"Sexual assault is a pretty serious breach of manners."

"Well, honestly, nobody knows if it really happened or not. I hate to say that, and I like Pomme but—"

"I must have been misled. I was told Pomme was your girlfriend. Is that not so?"

"My...?" He flushed in surprise. "No, I mean, we *were* in a relationship a few months ago which is why I know how... creative Pomme can be with the truth."

"Creative how?"

He ran a hand through his hair.

"I hate to do this. She's in so much trouble right now it feels wrong to speak out of school about her."

"It might actually help her."

"Okay, well, she didn't always tell the truth."

"Examples?"

"Okay, well, her husband? Who left her? I'm pretty sure he left her because she was sleeping around on him."

"Is that what Pomme told you?"

"Basically. She was still living with her husband when she and I were together."

"So, you know her kids?"

"No. She didn't want them thinking I was their new daddy or anything. Plus, they might tell her husband about me."

"Anything else?"

"I just feel like I'm throwing her under the bus, and I really care about her!"

"Just tell me what you know, please."

"I wasn't looking for a built-in family and anyway, possibly, Pomme was just a little too loose with her favors. You know the assault charge against Guy? One of the reasons Omar didn't take it seriously was because Pomme slept with *him* once, too."

I felt my heartbeat begin to speed up.

"Omar? You're saying Pomme slept with Omar Blanchet?" I asked.

"Please don't think badly of her. Pomme's a great girl.

Really. She's funny and smart and would do anything for you if you needed help."

"Do you think Omar didn't respect her complaint against Guy because he thought she was promiscuous?"

"You can hardly blame him. Since she also slept with Guy too."

17

I left my interview with Robert feeling totally
discombobulated. It seemed that Pomme had slept
with everyone, including the man she was accusing of
sexual assault. I'm not saying that was a game changer, but
the fact that she hadn't told me or her lawyer was problematic.

I put a call in to David asking if I could talk to Pomme
again, but he didn't answer, so I had to leave a message.
Then I went back to Cherise's apartment and although I
heard her little dog yap on the other side of the door,
nobody answered.

I was zero for zero today. I might as well try Mo Allard
again. I rang his office and talked to his secretary who told
me that he was in today but had no time to see anyone.

While it looked like my day was collapsing in a litany of
failed assignments, I am not one to waste a babysitter—
especially since I knew what kind of an exhausting evening I
had in store for me when I got home. At some point in the
morning when I was too distracted or tired to know what I

was doing, I had texted David and invited him for dinner. I'm not sure why I did that, but there you are. It was done.

On top of everything else I needed to do today, I also needed to pull together a dinner. And David was French. He would be expecting more than chicken in a bucket with a decent Merlot.

~

The cold wet weather had settled into a solid dull ache in my bones by the time I was standing in front of Omar and Liesel Blanchet's apartment building in Le Marais.

It occurred to me that I spend half my professional life ambushing suspects and witnesses in order to get answers to my questions. Mind you, I'd been trying to get an appointment with Mo Allard for three days now, which only served to underscore that walking up to a person's door and knocking on it unannounced was the best way to get what you wanted.

That is the reason I found myself once more at the apartment of Omar and Liesel Blanchet. I had no trouble slipping past the security door, since I was lucky enough to catch someone leaving. Most people didn't concern themselves with a sixty-something-year-old woman skipping the security code. They all just assumed that I'd forgotten it.

I checked the mailboxes in the foyer to find which one was Blanchet's, then went upstairs as confidently as if Madame Blanchet was expecting me. I really had nothing to lose by this gambit. If she talked, great. If she didn't, I was certainly no worse off than I was fifteen minutes ago.

I knocked on the door and it was opened by a sour-faced older woman in a maid's uniform. I was surprised since I didn't realize Omar was that wealthy, but also because most people's servants these days don't wear livery. That by itself told me something about the kind of person Liesel was.

"I am here to see Madame Blanchet," I said. "My name is Claire Baskerville."

"American?"

"As it happens."

The woman had me step inside, which I thought a very good sign, and then escorted me to the living room while she went to get Liesel.

The room she led me to was breathtaking in its scale—very unusual for an apartment in Paris. A towering wall of quartzite tiles reached from the carpet up to the rafters, making it the first thing you saw. Everything in the room was white or silver with a round mid-century modern coffee table in gold adding the only spot of color to an otherwise intensely themed décor.

One look at the ivory leather settee and I could not imagine curling up there with a throw and a hot cocoa.

Liesel came into the room, then. She was in her late thirties and very attractive. She had auburn curls and lively green eyes. Her complexion was clear—as all French women tend to be—but with a faint dusting of freckles.

We shook hands and she urged me to sit back down.

"You are an acquaintance of my husband?" she asked.

"I'm sorry, no," I said. "I never met him. I'm actually working with Pomme Toussaint's defense team."

"Ah, that is a sad business."

I was having trouble reading this woman. She seemed so pleasant and sincere that I instantly distrusted her.

"I was hoping you could answer a few questions for me. It might help her defense."

"If I can," she said. "Would you like a coffee?"

I could not remember a time when a suspect—especially one that I'd just barged in on—had offered me refreshments. Now I really did mistrust her.

"No, thank you," I said pleasantly. "I wanted to know if you knew that Guy Monet was your husband's biological son."

It wasn't until I laid eyes on the widow that I realized that there was no way she could be Guy's mother. They were too close in age. But I was still very keen to observe her reaction to my question.

"Oh, my goodness!" she said, her eyes wide in artifice and obvious deception. "No, I did not know that!"

Okay, so she already knew. One strike against the widow, I thought.

"Mama, can we play with the building blocks?"

I turned to see two small girls—twins—tiptoe into the room, holding hands.

Liesel's countenance softened and she smiled at them.

"Yes, of course, my darlings. But say hello, please, first."

"Bonjour, Madame."

"Bonjour, Madame."

"Bonjour," I said.

They were both completely adorable. Was it remotely possible that Liesel could have planned this? Ambushing me with cuteness in order to belay my natural tendency not to trust her? I chased the absurd notion from my mind.

"They are from my first marriage," Liesel said, smoothing out a nonexistent crease in her skirt and crossing her ankles. I saw her shoe soles and was shocked to see there was a hole in the bottom of one.

After the girls left, I told Liesel that I had changed my mind about coffee. I needed a moment to process this mysterious woman and her apartment and her servant.

Liesel excused herself to tell the uniformed maid to make coffee.

I looked around the room and saw what I had not seen before when I'd initially scanned the scene. Yes, it was beautiful and stylishly furnished. But the velvet on the chair arms was worn. Plus, there was a big stain on the ivory rug under the coffee table.

The thing that made me look deeper into my surroundings was the little girls. They were adorable and fresh-faced, scrubbed and rosy-cheeked. But their clothes were worn and in the case of one of the girls, too small for her. For that matter, now that I thought of it, Liesel herself was wearing a cashmere sweater that was pilling and jewelry that had to be costume jewelry—certainly not what I would've expected from the boss's wife.

Omar had only been dead a few days and this state of shabbiness had clearly been going on for longer than that. You never knew about people's marriages, as they often only allowed you to see what they wanted you to.

But it definitely raised the question: Was Liesel poor?

The rest of the visit was amiable and either Liesel really had nothing to tell me or she was a master manipulator. I left full of coffee and Christmas cookies that her girls had made and with not much more than a general feeling that even poor, she would probably be better off without her husband.

Although, especially in France, any family lawyer will tell you that—unless the wife were to inherit—the notion that she would be better off without her husband was just absurd.

18

On my way home from the Blanchet neighborhood, I walked down Boulevard Haus-mann to enjoy the lights and decorations that the high-end boutiques put up around Rue Faubourg-St-Honoré and Avenue Montagne. I had read that Place Vendôme was decorated with over two hundred pine trees and that the Bercy Village entertainment district had installed a thousand twinkling umbrellas.

As I walked past the amazing display windows at *Galeries Lafayette* with their astonishingly realistic village motifs, I got a text from David. To read it, I stepped out of the tide of tourists—which was much heavier around the department store than anywhere else on the street.

David said he'd be delighted to come to dinner and that he'd bring the wine. I was glad he was coming—even if bringing the wine was literally the least he could do. I hated to spoil my good mood but when Jean-Marc came to dinner he usually brought the ingredients and cooked it too. What's that line about not knowing how good you have it until it's gone? Yeah, that.

"I have some news," David said. "Documents were subpoenaed from Liesel Blanchet's attorney that showed she had already started the attempt to get the will overturned in her favor—a week before Omar died."

"Uh oh, that sounds fishy," I said.

Again, French inheritance law is very strict. It was the children who inherited, and they inherited equally. None of this I-liked-my-youngest-best stuff. The spouse unfortunately was SOL—or whatever the French cognate for that was.

I told David that I'd just spent an hour with Liesel Blanchet and he was excited to hear all about it at dinner tonight. As we signed off, it occurred to me that one good thing about sort-of-dating a work colleague was that you never had to worry about what to talk about.

I tucked my phone away and headed back down Boulevard Hausmann to hit the delicatessen just a few blocks from my apartment. They did a lovely roast chicken smothered in rosemary and all I had to do was hide the packaging and make a nice risotto.

As I burrowed deeper into my coat, noting the snow flurries as they once more danced in front of me, I thought that one thing I knew if I knew anything was that once Liesel discovered that Guy was her husband's legal son—*and make no mistake, she knew*—she'd have known her chances of beating both him *and* Cherise were much less likely.

More like impossible.

In my book, that made Liesel Blanchet my number one biggest contender for Guy's murder.

19

I got back that afternoon in time to take Izzy for a quick walk around the block before my sitter vamoosed. I also allowed myself a few moments to snuggle on the couch with Maddie, Robbie and Izzy while Christmas carols played on the HomePod so that Robbie could tell me about his day with the new sitter. He liked her well enough but reported that she didn't play like Haley did.

Since the sitter was probably in her forties, I imagine he meant by that, that the woman didn't happily race up and down the stairs with him, throw a ball in the courtyard or spend endless hours pushing him on the swing in a frozen park the way Haley would have. But they were both alive. So, I called it a win.

After settling Robbie on the floor in the living room with some puzzles—this time with the TV off—I fed Maddie in her bouncer chair on the dining room table.

It's typically when I'm doing mundane, nonskilled tasks like this that my mind skitters away to mull over things I don't think of the rest of the day—except when I'm trying to fall asleep at night of course. Then, my mind is only too happy to consider at great length any manner of trivial thing that happened to me that day.

But this evening—with dinner prep basically consisting of reheating the chicken, spooning up the risotto that I bought at Monoprix on the way home, and releasing the salad from its plastic bag—I spooned a mushy combination of carrots and beets into Maddie's willing mouth and found myself reflecting on the things I'd done and learned today.

First but not at all foremost was the fact of my visit with Liesel. I wanted to like her but couldn't help but admit I'd found her suspicious. She was definitely lying about not knowing about Guy being Omar's biological son. And if she *was* poor, that would be a motive for her to step up her game to get that inheritance from Cherise and Guy. Would that involve murder?

I forced myself to ignore her friendliness and her two adorable children, because she was definitely my best bet for a murder suspect.

On the other hand, there was the fact that Pomme also seemed to have lied to me. She told me her connection with Robert had been a one-night stand but Robert said it was a *relationship*.

So, who is telling the truth?

Worse than that was Robert's news that Pomme had slept with Omar Blanchet and also the man she'd accused of sexually assaulting her. If true, it was very discouraging. On the other hand, I couldn't just take Robert's word for it. Not when it would be so easy to verify.

I stepped into the living room to check on Robbie but he was still happily singing along to the carols and playing with his puzzles. Maddie was done eating, so I wiped her down and untied her bib and put her on the floor in her bouncy chair with Robbie and Izzy. Izzy would finish cleaning the baby up of her dinner and keep her amused in the process.

I went back to the kitchen to put away baby food jars and to check the time. Even if I had time for a quick bath—I didn't—I couldn't leave Robbie and Maddie on their own. Instead, I pulled out my laptop from the bookcase in the dining room and settled down for a quick snoop around Pomme's social media page.

Within ten minutes I had my answer.

Pomme's social media pages were equal parts posts about her two little boys and her own very active social life. While I didn't find any posts of her with men during the time her husband lived at home—she at least had that much sense—there were plenty of photos of her draped over men's laps since then.

There was even a photo of her with her arm around Guy, both of them with drunken glazes and glasses of champagne in their hands at a Christmas party two years ago. I closed my laptop and felt emotionally conflicted.

I *liked* Pomme and I really wanted to help her. But it looked very much like she was not only promiscuous but a liar.

The question now was, was she also a murderer?

20

D avid arrived a few minutes early and when I opened the door, I actually felt a shot of delight to see him. He had an armful of gaily wrapped packages and I couldn't help but be charmed by how thoughtful that was.

He even brought a chew bone with a bow on it for Izzy.

If I was wondering if this evening was all-business or a date, I wondered no more.

As Robbie gleefully ripped apart the paper on his gift, I went to uncork the wine that David had brought. I could hear him talking with Robbie and wondered if he had children of his own. Since he was probably in his fifties, he probably had grandchildren of his own.

I joined him in the living room with two glasses of wine.

"How did you know exactly what four-year-old boys want?" I asked with a smile.

David took one of the drinks from me.

"I've got one about that age," he said and then laughed. "I mean, my daughter does."

I wondered what he thought about the fact that I had

Robbie at my age. Usually, one of the benefits of being in your sixties is that all the child-rearing business is behind you, and you can launch off for weekend jaunts any time you please. Although, of course, with Izzy, I had never been quite that free.

"Does your ex-wife live in Paris?" I asked as we watched Robbie attempt to show Maddie his new truck.

I don't know why I asked that. Sometimes I just get into interrogation mode and forget to stop. Thankfully, David didn't seem to mind.

"No, she's in London."

Right about then I could smell the *gougères* were ready to come out of the oven, so I excused myself to get them before they burned. He followed me into the kitchen.

"Do the kiddies need watching?" he asked. "Or can we talk?"

I turned to look at him and quickly realized he meant about the case.

"They're fine for now," I said as I slid the cheese puffs onto a plate and led the way to the dining table which earlier I'd had Robbie set for dinner. We sat down with our drinks. I led off the discussion by telling him about my visit with Liesel and how I'd found her almost too nice and disarming—as if she were acting very hard to come across that way.

He frowned.

"I admit Liesel has motive," he said. "Especially if she's hurting financially as you suspect."

"It's Pomme I'm worried about," I said. "She's not telling us the truth."

"Well, not the whole truth anyway, I agree."

"I know that a prior sexual relationship with her assailant doesn't mean she wasn't sexually attacked by him."

"No, but it makes it harder to prove, that's for sure. Especially if it comes before a jury."

"Well, we don't have to worry about that now," I said.

"True, but it's still damning. In fact, more so because we don't have Guy Monet walking around being an ass and corroborating her claims by his actions. It's worse than he-said-she-said because the *he* in this equation is dead."

He popped a second *gougère* in his mouth. "These are great, by the way."

"Thanks. It just worries me that Pomme isn't telling us the truth."

"Most clients don't," he said with a shrug. "I guess I'm used to it. By the way, have you had a chance to talk to Omar's partner yet?"

"Mo Allard? No. And I've tried for days now."

Out of the corner of my eye I could see Maddie was squirming and I knew I'd have to check on her in a moment to see how dry she was.

"In a normal situation," David said with a sigh, "the police would bring him in for questioning. But I don't think they'll bother now. They think they have the case wrapped up with Pomme."

"Why? What's happened?"

"It appears they discovered a letter on Allard's computer from Guy Monet saying he would not honor a debt to Mo once he inherited."

"Whoa, wait. A debt?"

"Do you want the last one?" he asked as his hand hovered over the cheese puff plate. I shook my head.

"Omar Blanchet borrowed fifty thousand euros from Allard a year ago," he said.

"That's a lot of money to lose. Especially when you know

the guy left holding all the money has no intention of honoring the debt."

"It's even worse than that," David said. "The cops have a witness who claims she heard Cherise tell Omar that *she* would honor the debt if she inherited."

"So, you think Cherise and Allard are working together?"

David laughed. "I'm not thinking anything. It's just a little suspicious, is all."

"Does Monsieur Allard have an alibi for the night Guy was killed?"

"A very weak one. The cops haven't pushed on it, but it'll collapse if they try."

I clenched my jaw in frustration.

Why weren't the police talking to Mo Allard? He has motive out the derriere!

"What's his alibi?"

"He claims he was at the movies."

"Where?"

"Avenue Mac-Mahon."

"That's close to the Christmas markets!"

"A three-minute walk. I know. So do the police."

"And they're still not going to bring him in?"

"No. Are you ready for one more strike against him?"

"I don't think I can bear it. But go on."

"Turns out he has a gun collection."

21

The rest of the night was lovely. Robbie sat still for his portion of dinner and when it was time for his bath—Maddie didn't officially go down for an hour past his bedtime—David stepped outside with Izzy so she could wet the courtyard pavers and he could have a cigarette.

It took me a few bedtime stories longer than usual to get Robbie to drop off so that by the time I returned to the living room, David was sitting on the couch watching a Christmas movie on mute with Maddie in the crook of his arm and Izzy nestled next to his hip.

I loved seeing that, of course, which was all the more confusing when it made me realize that seeing him like that made me miss Jean-Marc all the more for some reason. I'm not sure it was fair to David, considering the effort he was putting in to being the perfect date, but my heart didn't want someone new. My heart wanted someone irascible and stubborn and often downright impossible to reason with. Go figure.

"I think this one is ready to drop off, too," he said as I

came and relieved him of Maddie. "I don't know how you do it."

He meant *at your age,* but I let it go. After all, he wasn't wrong. Taking care of two kids under the age of five was exhausting no matter how old you were.

I sat down on the couch beside him. I still needed to give Maddie a last feeding and then, if not a bath, at least a top and tail.

Just thinking about it made me want to crawl under the mohair throw on the couch and call it a day. Instead, I took in another breath, gathered what wisps of energy I had left, and stood up.

"I won't be long," I promised.

"I'll wait," he said, smiling up at me with a gorgeous pair of brown eyes that someone, if they weren't careful, could totally fall face-first into.

I hesitated before stepping away.

"David," I said. "Is it possible...I mean, do you think I could talk to Pomme again? Like tomorrow? I'm on her team as much as you are, but I really can't rest until I hear what she has to say."

He grinned at me. "How does twenty minutes sound?"

I gave him a blank look and he held up his phone.

"I'd already called in a favor at the holding facility. You're not the only one who wants answers, Claire."

"Seriously?" I felt a thrum of excitement rush through me at the thought of talking to Pomme.

"Don't rush," he said, nodding at the baby. "I've got a few questions for her myself and they'll let us have a good fifteen minutes."

By the time I fed, bathed and got Maddie down in her

crib, I came back to the living room to see David on his cellphone. He looked up at me and held up a finger.

"Okay, Pomme," he said. "Just let me know if it happens again. Meanwhile, I'll talk to the *Inspecteur Principale*."

That didn't sound good and made me pause, since I'd planned that my conversation with Pomme would be mildly assertive. David covered the receiver.

"Did you confront her about the Facebook posts?" I whispered.

"No. I thought I'd leave that to you."

"Is everything okay with her at the jail?"

"As okay as can be expected, considering it's a jail," he said.

I grimaced and took the phone.

"Pomme? This is Claire."

"Yes, Claire. And even in jail, this is late."

Her tone and comment erased any hesitancy I'd had about pulling my punches.

"Sorry to interrupt your evening," I said and wished I'd bitten my tongue. She was in jail for heaven's sakes. Sarcasm was not warranted, no matter how annoyed I was with her.

"What is it you want?" she asked.

"I want to know about the photograph of you and Guy Monet I found on the Internet. It looks like the two of you were an item. It looks like you were together."

"That's why you wanted to talk to me? At ten o'clock at night?" She snorted loudly. "It was just one night. Maybe two."

"And it was consensual?"

"It was."

When I didn't immediately respond, Pomme added hotly: "Don't tell me. You don't think someone can assault you if you willingly slept with them before? I'm sure that's

what Guy's defense attorney would have said too. Are you
sure you're on the right team?"

This woman really made it hard to like her, let alone go
the extra mile for her.

"Of course not, Pomme," I said tightly, "but keeping it a
secret—and one that had little hope of *staying* secret—
undermines your credibility and your lawyer's ability to do
his job."

"My very life undermines my credibility," Pomme said
bitterly. "Anything else?"

Before I could answer, she'd disconnected. I'd wanted to
ask her about her relationship with Robert and sleeping
with Omar but after hitting her with my big gun—her relationship with Guy—I guess she figured the conversation
could only go downhill from there.

She was probably right.

I handed the phone back to David.

"You're getting another call," I said before he could ask
me how my call with Pomme went.

I sat down on the couch while David took his call. I'm
not sure how I expected to feel after talking to her. Or what
I'd expected her to do. She couldn't deny her relationship
with Guy, since I had the Facebook photos as proof. I guess I
was hoping she'd have been a little more contrite. Instead of
making me feel better, I felt tons worse. And not just about
how Pomme spoke to me, but how I now had to face something I saw in myself. Something I didn't like at all. I realized
that I found it hard to view someone as promiscuous and
also comfortable with lying, and still be able to see the best
in them.

Very hard.

David moved to the dining room with his phone call and
I saw he was pacing and getting agitated. Izzy jumped off

the couch and ran to him, even barking once, although they'd gotten along so well earlier in the evening.

Something was wrong. I could sense it. I felt an ache develop in the back of my throat.

When David hung up, he just stood in my dining room staring at his phone as if he'd forgotten what it was for. Then he turned to look at me, his face a canvas of shock and dismay.

He rubbed his jaw over and over again.

"David, what's happened?" I said getting up to walk over to him.

I felt dread and misgiving climb up into my chest. Something bad was coming. He shook his head as if trying to dislodge something from his brain.

"You're not going to believe this," he said.

I took his hand. "What's happened?"

I had visions of Pomme hanging up the phone from me and somehow hanging herself and, as horrible as that image was, I wasn't far wrong.

"It's Cherise," he said, his eyes glazed in shock. "She's been murdered."

22

Suffice to say, news of Cherise Blanchet's murder had put the kibosh on the rest of our dinner date. Although neither David nor I had a stake in what happened to Cherise, we both felt gutted with the news. And of course, it was all very well to say it had nothing to do with Pomme's case, but that didn't mean Cherise's death wasn't connected to Omar or Guy's death.

So, yes, of course, it was connected to Pomme's case. David and I just didn't know how yet.

The next morning, after I settled Robbie, Maddie and Izzy with the same interim babysitter, I grabbed a coffee to go from my favorite *boulangerie*—and a croissant for nourishment—and hurried over to Cherise's apartment. I'd planned on meeting David there, but he texted me when I was enroute to say he couldn't make it because one of his other clients was having a meltdown. I couldn't imagine doing what David did for a living. He represented the poorest of the poor and, honestly, he did it even if they were guilty.

I think David was good at his job, but there was no

doubt it was high stress with an even higher fail rate. A lesser man would get burned out pretty quickly, I imagined.

As soon as I made it to Cherise's neighborhood, I could see that the cops were still there processing the crime scene. They had barricaded off one lane of the street in front of Cherise's apartment. Three police vans were parked ominously in the middle of the road. I didn't see an ambulance or coroner's wagon and it had been at least ten hours, so I was relatively sure the body had been taken away. A small crowd was gathered in front of the building.

Detective Monique Semple stood out front with her notepad and her customary scowl as she glowered at an older woman wearing a long dark wool coat and carrying a shopping bag. Today was Wednesday, a popular day for the area produce and fish markets. This woman looked as if she had been on her way to the markets. As surreptitiously as I could, I sidled up to the other side of her.

"...live on the other side of Mademoiselle Blanchet," the old woman was saying. "But I answered all these questions last night when you people came to my door."

"I understand, Madame Mordot," Semple said, her voice clearly communicating that understanding and caring were two very different things. "But we need to ask them again. You mentioned you saw someone leave Mademoiselle Blanchet's apartment last night?"

The old woman sighed with annoyance.

"Yes, yes. I heard screaming—"

"Wait. You heard screaming? My notes said it was arguing."

"Yes, Madame Agent, it was a screaming argument. Okay?"

"Continue."

"I opened my door to tell Mademoiselle Blanchet to

keep the noise down and I saw a woman leave her apartment which surprised me because the screaming I heard was not two women."

"You heard a man and a woman arguing?"

"That's right."

"Can you describe the woman you saw?"

"She wore a hat pulled down low over her face so don't ask me to come and sit with a sketch artist! As it is, I'm missing all the best fish at the markets!"

"Do you remember anything else?"

"She carried a Hermès bag."

That comment stopped me because if the mystery woman was trying to be incognito, carrying a fifteen-hundred-euro bag was hardly the way to do it. But then maybe the killer wasn't very smart.

"Thank you, Madame Mordot," Semple said. Before I had a chance to slip unseen into the crowd, the detective called out to me.

"What are you doing here, Madame Baskerville?" she asked. "You are worse than lawyers hoping to find a lawsuit on the ground."

This woman was always so unpleasant to me. But because of what I did for a living, I couldn't afford to alienate her. At least not too much.

"I was only curious, Madame Agent," I said pleasantly. Then, because I knew it would only anger her to be blown off when I obviously had a reason to be here, I hurriedly continued. "Mademoiselle Blanchet was a key figure in a case I'm working."

"The Guy Monet case," she said, curling her lip in disgust.

"Yes, that's right. May I assume Mademoiselle Blanchet's death was not accidental?"

"You may assume what you like," she said, jamming her folded notebook into her jacket pocket. "As long as you stay out of my way."

I gave her my best, most obsequious nod and then turned to escape when I saw David arriving at the scene in a taxi. I hurried over to him.

"I didn't think you were going to be able to make it," I said.

He smiled at me as if just the sight of my face had made his whole day, then leaned over and kissed me on both cheeks.

"I was able to get free," he said. "Anything to learn here?"

I turned to look at the fluttering police tape across the front of the building entrance.

"Not unless you can get us inside to the crime scene," I said.

He put his hand on my arm and steered me down the street.

"No, but I know a place that makes their own *canelés*," he said.

An hour later, we were sitting in a charming *brasserie* with hand-stitched banquettes, wicker-backed chairs and the kind of homespun Parisian charm that is touted on all the most popular travel sites. The foam on my cappuccino was high and dusted with cinnamon and fragrant with cardamon. And David wasn't wrong about the *canelés*. They were exquisite.

"I overheard Semple taking a statement from one of the neighbors," I said as I dumped another packet of sugar into my coffee. "She said she saw a woman leave but she had no details beyond the fact that she carried a Hermès bag."

"Half the women in Paris carry Hermès," he said.

"I wish!" I said, and then blushed. "Oh, you're probably right." I got mine from a consignment store for under a thousand, but it was in mint condition, and I carry it every chance I got.

"The police will check the usual suspects," he said. "And see who has an alibi and who doesn't."

"What usual suspects?" but as soon as I said it, I realized there was only one obvious answer to the question: *who would kill Cherise?*

It was Liesel Blanchet on all counts.

With both of Omar's children dead, Liesel would now inherit without question. That unfortunately was motive in spades for killing Cherise.

"Do you have any details of the murder itself?" I asked.

"Stabbed," he said. "Murder weapon in the apartment. And then some."

"What does *and then some* mean?" I asked with a frown.

The holiday decorations in the *brasserie* were minimal but elegant. Just seeing all the mahogany paneling draped in tasteful green velvet swags gave me a sense of peace.

"It means the police also uncovered the murder weapon from Guy's murder. With Cherise's fingerprints on it."

"That's great! So why is Pomme still being held?"

"The police think there's something odd about the prints," David said, signaling to the waiter for another plate of *canelés*.

"Odd how?"

"The ME thinks someone put Cherise's fingerprints on the gun post-mortem."

"And they think Liesel did that?" I asked. "Do they really think she's capable of doing something like that?"

"Well, they think she murdered someone in cold blood, so yeah," he said.

"But what do they have that might point to that?"

David's shoulders slumped and he pushed away his pastry, no longer hungry.

"They think she was probably the mystery woman seen at Cherise's apartment that night."

"Based on what? The neighbor said she couldn't identify the woman."

"They've got other things to go on."

"Like what?"

"Like the fact that her fingerprints were found on the knife that killed Cherise."

23

That afternoon, after David made a few phone calls, he succeeded in talking with Liesel on the phone and she eagerly accepted his offer of help of representation. So, a few hours after leaving Cherise's apartment, I found myself sitting in a police interview room with David and a very distraught Liesel Blanchet sitting across from us.

Gone was the soft look of general worry and vague hope I thought I'd seen in her before. Now her freckles stood out like she'd been spattered with a paint brush. Her face was so pale, her eyes looked gaunt and haunted. I was relieved to see that at least she hadn't been handcuffed for our meeting.

"Have you given a statement to the police?" David asked.

She promptly burst into tears which I feared meant she had. That wasn't the end of the world if she was innocent, but that fact had yet to be proven to me and David. I glanced at him as he handed her a tissue. Would he still represent her if it turned out she killed Cherise? I felt completely sure he would.

"Why don't you tell us what happened?" he asked.

Sniffling and shredding the tissue with her tears, Liesel worked to pull herself together.

"I didn't kill her," she said.

Always a good start, I thought, giving David a hopeful look.

"What happened?" David prodded.

The fact was, finding out that Liesel's fingerprints had been found on the murder weapon was discouraging to the say the least. And unlike the gun with Cherise's prints on it, these prints had been forensically confirmed as authentic.

Liesel Blanchet had held the knife that killed Cherise.

Pretty damning.

Now we just had to hope she had an ironclad alibi for the time of murder.

"I went to her apartment to talk to her," she said.

My heart sank. There went the alibi.

"Did you tell the police this?" I asked.

She nodded miserably.

"I wanted to ask her—to beg her, really—to allow me a tiny portion of Omar's estate. Just a bit! I needed it for my girls. He left me with nothing!"

"Neighbors reported hearing shouting coming from Cherise's apartment," David said.

She nodded miserably.

"We argued. It was terrible. I couldn't believe she would let us go with nothing. Ilse and Ingrid are her nieces!"

Step-nieces, I thought. To some people, that was no relation at all.

"They found your fingerprints on the knife that killed Cherise," David said softly.

Liesel began to weep. I could see she was crying, not out of guilt or misery at being found out, but in genuine frustration because she was not going to be believed. The physical forensics told a story that belied anything she could say.

"I picked up a paring knife from the counter," she said, taking another tissue from David. "But I wasn't going to use it on her! Things started to get very dramatic and that's all it was. I never threatened her with it. I just waved it around before stabbing it into her butcher block counter. It was just for emphasis!"

As she worked again to overcome her emotion, I felt a sadness ripple through me. It was heartbreaking that both Pomme and Liesel were in jail. Before we came into the interview, David had been informed that Liesel's two little girls were currently in care awaiting the arrival of their father from Germany—a man whom Liesel claimed was an abusive ex-spouse.

I couldn't get over how my own Christmas was being defined by two separate cases—both involving mothers torn from their children. So far, nothing that Liesel had told us seemed connected in any way to Guy's murder. And if Cherise's death didn't change the facts surrounding Guy's murder, then Pomme was still on the hook for it.

I glanced at David. While I knew he wanted to help Liesel, I also knew he was hoping to find some connection between the two cases. He was hoping that one might give insight into the other.

And that at least one of the mothers might be found innocent.

"Did you know that Guy Monet was Omar's son?" I asked.

Liesel wiped her eyes and let out a long sigh.

"Yes," she said.

"How long had you known?"

"Omar told me after we were married."

That meant she'd known for years. And *years* was plenty of time to plan something for when your husband died so that your stepson didn't inherit. Or at least that's what the state's prosecution would say.

"How well did you know Guy Monet?" David asked.

"Not well," she said. "Omar loved him, but he never came to the house. I knew he slept around, and that Omar wasn't happy about that."

"Did you hear about him and Pomme Toussaint?" I asked.

She nodded. "Just gossip. I don't think they were ever formally together."

"So just a fling?" I asked.

She shrugged. "I guess."

"Did Omar know?"

"I doubt it. He wouldn't have been happy at all to hear Guy was dating the girl who flipped *crêpes* on the street."

That pinged something in the back of my brain and I didn't know why. While David continued to talk, I wrestled with what Liesel's comment might have meant, but nothing became clear.

"Can you see if Greta is okay?" Liesel asked us suddenly.

I frowned and David went looking through his notes as if looking for a reference to a Greta.

"Our maid," Liesel said. "She was so worried when the police arrested me this morning."

The maid was worried?

"I had told her to go buy some clothes," Liesel said, her voice shaking, "and when she came back, the police were there, taking me and the girls away."

"Why was Greta buying clothes?" I asked.

Liesel took in a breath and wiped away the last of her tears.

"I hated that Omar made her wear that ridiculous maid's costume. If she and I were anywhere near the same size, I would've just let her go through my closet. As it was, I told her to find something she liked and put it on my card."

I will happily admit when I'm wrong about someone. Okay, maybe not *happily*, but yes, I was wrong about Liesel thinking she was to-the-manor-born. The more I talked to her, the more I could see that my initial impression of her had been correct. She was down to earth and basically kind.

I hate it when nice people fool me like that and they really *are* nice, but I'm so immersed in the unsavory bits of my profession that I often can't see it.

Note to self: Quit being so cynical.

"One last question," I said. "Did Cherise know Pomme?"

"Of course." Liesel frowned. "They worked for the same company for nearly a year. Why would you think they didn't?"

Why indeed. Pomme swore she'd never met Cherise. Lies. Again. Lies.

When the guards came into the interview room to tell us our time was up, I impulsively gave Liesel a hug. The French aren't big into hugs, but she was German and I thought she might appreciate it. The saddest thing that has happened to me this month was the past thirty minutes and I hoped very much that David and I were going to be able to help her.

As we left the room, I heard David getting a text. He read it as we walked into the waiting room.

"What is it?" I asked.

"The cops have just destroyed Mo Allard's alibi," he said.

"For Guy's murder?"

"And also Cherise's. Regardless of what Cherise said publicly about honoring her father's debt, we don't know the whole story."

"This is great!" I said. "Because Mo Allard already had motive and opportunity!"

David put his phone away and I could tell by his affect, that he didn't think anything about this was even remotely great.

"David, what is it?" I asked in growing dread and frustration.

"Because the police have Liesel's prints on the murder weapon, they aren't going forward with any investigation into Mo Allard."

The disappointment was like a bitter taste in the back of my throat.

As we left the headquarters, I saw that it had started to snow again. I realized at that moment that I probably felt just as discouraged at David did. The sad truth was, if the police weren't going to investigate this case any further—*and if Liesel didn't kill Cherise*—then someone was going to get away with murder.

24

I t was late afternoon by the time I parted company with David after we left the police station. We made a lackluster suggestion to get together in a few days to take Robbie sledding in the park. I felt discouraged and beat down. Both Pomme and Liesel would be spending Christmas away from their children. It made me want to rush home and give Robbie and Maddie big hugs. And Catherine and my little grandson Cameron. I wondered when I'd ever see Cam again and realized I missed him terribly.

I have to say that whenever I feel hopeless or disappointed, I find that taking action of almost any kind often helps. That's why, as I was glumly plodding home, unmindful of the beautiful street decorations all around me, I looked around and realized that I was a mere two blocks from OmniManger and Mo Allard's office,

I texted the babysitter to make sure everything was fine on that front and then received a text from Geneviève reminding me to pick up cereal at Monoprix for Robbie. I looked up at the thick bands of clouds that hung oppressively overhead and shivered.

Maybe I'd treat myself to a hot mulled wine at the Tuileries Garden Christmas Market. It was on my way home —now that I was going home by way of Omar and Mo's business.

~

The office building of OmniManger was an ugly block of windowless cement but was at least far enough away from the usual tourist routes so as not to serve as a blight to the casual observer.

The one good thing about blindsiding someone who works in a public office is that you generally don't have to sneak through security gates or past some eagle-eyed on-duty concierge. I walked right into the office and took the lobby elevator up to the floor that housed OmniManger, grateful that the office wasn't closed yet for the holidays.

When I walked into the company's lobby, I was gratified to see that the waiting room was bare—and so was the receptionist's desk. This was the day before Christmas Eve and likely the office Christmas party was happening some place off site and the employees had left hours earlier.

But there was always one person who would take advantage of the quiet and the lack of ringing phones. That person was usually the man who paid the bills to keep the lights on. As I stepped in the hallway, I wasn't surprised to see an open door with light spilling out at the end of the hall and a plaque on the door that read *President*.

I made my way silently down the hall and stood in the office doorway. He sat hunched over his laptop on his desk, a mug of something on the blotter before him. He had grey hair and a barrel chest to go with his beefy powerful arms.

Although I hadn't moved, it was just a few seconds before Mo felt eyes on him and looked up. Instantly he stiffened and sat straight up, his face pinched with annoyance. I have to admit, he couldn't be blamed for thinking nobody would bother him tonight of all nights. I stepped into the office and took a seat in one of the leather chairs that faced his desk.

"Who are you? What are you doing here?"

"Joyeux Noël to you too, Monsieur Allard," I said. "I'm here for our appointment."

"What appointment?"

"The one I've been trying to make with you for the past three days."

"I don't know what you're talking about."

"I'm talking about five minutes of your time on behalf of Pomme Toussaint who is sitting in jail right this minute on what I think you know is a bogus charge."

He crossed his arms and pinched his lips together as if I'd have to pry them open to get anything out of him.

"I'm not sure I know that at all," he said.

"So you think Pomme set out to murder Guy Monet?"

He hesitated. "Who are you again?"

"My name is Claire Baskerville and I'm working with the public defender's office on Pomme's case. I only need a few minutes of your time. Please."

He tossed down his pen.

"I'm sure I can be of no help," he said.

"Let me decide that. Have the police talked to you about your alibi?"

"My what?" He flushed and ran a hand through his hair. "What about it?"

"They've broken it, Monsieur Allard. The movie you went to? Nobody can confirm seeing you there."

"That's not my problem!"

"Actually, it is. The burden of proof of innocence is on you, I'm afraid. And even if you do scrape up someone who'll admit to seeing you, that particular movie house is only a three-minute walk from the Christmas market."

"So?" But his face quickly changed when he realized what I was suggesting. "Nobody thinks I killed Guy! Why would I? What possible reason would I have?"

"An email was found on Guy's computer that was sent to you saying he would not honor the debt Omar had to you."

Allard blinked. He raised his hand as if to bite his nails and then quickly thought better of it.

"Look, I didn't kill Guy, if that's what you're implying," he said, but the energy had been stripped from his voice. His eyes darted around the room as if he was already envisioning a life behind bars.

"Did you know Cherise Blanchet?"

He whitened at the mention of her name which told me he'd heard of her recent death.

Or was the cause of it.

"Of course, I know Cherise. She was Omar's daughter."

"Did you know Pomme Toussaint?" I asked while I had him on the ropes.

"I'm sure I met her," he said, wiping a bead of sweat from his upper lip. "But she didn't work in the office. I think she was dating Omar's PA."

"You're referring to Robert Granger?"

Mo grimaced, but he nodded.

"Don't you like Robert?" I asked.

"It's not that," he said. "I hardly said two words to him. It's just..." He paused and then clearly decided not to hold back. "Robert asked me for a promotion the day after Omar died. I didn't love the timing. Pretty crass considering he was Omar's personal assistant."

"What did you tell him?"

"He caught me at a bad time," he said. "I was probably a little blunter with him than I should've been."

"So you turned him down?"

"Look, by rights he should've been let go as soon as Omar died. I held off, thinking I might find something for him to do. I'm not heartless. And I always felt bad for the guy. Being raised in foster care, he hasn't had many breaks."

I felt a coldness ripple through me.

Robert said he'd had a close relationship with his father.

"Robert was in foster care?"

"I shouldn't have told you that. I'm sure that's privileged information or something. Can you forget I mentioned it?"

"Sure. So did you find something for Robert to do now that Omar was gone?"

He cleared his throat and gave a shrug that looked not one bit natural.

"I told him I'd think about it. He came to me right after Cherise stormed in here saying she was an equal partner and things were going to change. I could hardly give Robert an answer with things so up in the air."

Mo was sweating again. And the look he gave me told me what he didn't need to say in words. And that was that he very much wished he hadn't mentioned that Cherise had come to him after Guy was killed.

Because her threatening to change things with the company had to look a whole lot like motive to anyone with a brain.

25

Walking away from Mo's office, I could see the glow and movement of the carousel in the Jardin des Tuileries. It had been on my list to take Robbie there this year, but we never made it. I watched the colorful lights of the merry-go-round and tried to imagine the happy faces of the children who must be riding it on Christmas Eve.

I sighed and turned away from the sight, heading to the nearest Metro. It was too cold to walk and I was tired. Aside from the fact that I'd left Monsieur Allard a quivering pile of insecurity and fear, what I hadn't picked up from him was guilt. Now I know a lot of people pooh-pooh the ability of intuition for that sort of thing. And honestly Jean-Marc and I had had long conversations on this very topic. But the fact is, the way I see it, guilt is like lying or fear.

If you see enough of it, you can detect it. I'll go to my grave believing that.

And as edgy and nervous as Mo Allard behaved, I did not detect guilt on him.

Now, granted, a true sociopath doesn't give off fear or

guilt vibes and they—and thank goodness sociopaths are rare—can throw an investigator's natural instinct or intuition straight into the crapper.

But Mo Allard wasn't a sociopath. He was a businessman. And along with that, he may be ruthless and perfectly capable of dissembling or lying, murder was a long jump from those.

I remembered that I'd intended to treat myself to a hot wine before going home, so I stopped at the next café I came to. Like everywhere else in Paris, it was gaily decorated for the season with glittering gold ornaments swinging from the eaves.

My waiter brought me my hot wine which is virtually a staple in France at Christmas time. Made with dry red wine, sugar, orange and fragrant spices like cinnamon, star anise, cardamon and cloves, it is a beverage to truly warm you up inside and out.

As I sipped my wine, enjoying its heady fragrance, I saw a line of heavy-coated musicians, many toting their instruments, walking in the direction of Sainte-Chapelle which was next door to the police station. I'd taken Robbie to Sainte-Chapelle's famous and truly indelible Christmas Eve concert last year. He'd been too young at the time to really appreciate the music but when the light from the dropping sun hit the chapel's famous stained-glass windows, they literally glowed and Robbie had clapped his hands in delight. Honestly so did half the audience, most of them grown-ups.

Suddenly, I felt that same ping that had occurred when Liesel commented this morning about how Omar wouldn't have liked Guy dating "that girl that worked the *crêpe* pan." Something began to take form in my brain.

Have I been looking at the wrong motivation all along?

Just like everyone else, I assumed Guy's murder was about money. But what if it wasn't? Every one of our suspects with the exception of Pomme and Robert had a motive to kill him related to money. But those two didn't. Neither were expected to inherit. Neither were expected to profit from Guy's death.

What if Guy had been killed for a reason other than the money?

I called David.

"Miss me already?" he said with a throaty laugh.

That was such a sexy, boyfriend thing to say that I didn't know how to respond. So I ignored it.

"What if Guy was killed for another reason besides money?"

"Like what kind of reason?"

Jealousy. Envy. Revenge.

"Do we know if Guy knew he was Omar's bio son?"

"Uncertain."

"Who did know?"

"For sure Liesel and of course Cherise. Possibly Mo."

"How about his personal assistant?"

"Most definitely."

The more attention I paid to the picture that was forming in my head, the more chilled I became.

"David, can you meet me? I know it's late."

It wasn't late. But it was the day before Christmas Eve.

"Are you serious?" he asked.

"We need to do this tonight."

"Do what?"

"Please, David? It's important."

"Okay, fine. But I can't stay long. I'm supposed to take the train home."

"Where's home?"

"Lyons."

"What time's your train?"

"Nineteen hundred hours."

I glanced at my watch. His train left at seven o'clock and it was just a little before five now.

"No problem," I said, knowing that if everything went as I thought it might there was absolutely no way David was going to make that train.

And probably not tomorrow either.

26

P aris in the winter means it's generally dark by four o'clock. I've lived here four years and I'm still not used to it. It meant however that the little pocket park in front of Robert Granger's building felt even less inviting at this time of day than the first time I saw it.

I didn't even know for a fact that he was home. I was pretty sure he didn't have any family to go home to over the holidays and I was betting that he had a habit of treating Christmas like any other day. I'd read that was what a lot of foster kids did when the holidays hadn't been exactly the best part of their year.

There was nobody in the park except an elderly woman with a small dog. She gave me several suspicious looks since I was loitering in a park with no obvious reason for being there. As soon as I spotted David coming through the entrance, I figured she would probably relax thinking I was just waiting for an assignation.

David hurried over to me. Despite the purpose of our meeting—which I still had yet to reveal to David—we kissed in greeting. His cheek was ice cold, and I wondered if he'd taken the Metro from his office or if he'd walked.

"I am extremely curious and not a little bit flattered," he said with a grin.

I nodded at the building in front of us.

"That's Robert Granger's apartment building," I said.

"And why are we at Robert Granger's apartment building?"

"Because I'm almost positive he killed Guy and also Cherise."

David's smile slid from his face. "What are you talking about? And why couldn't we discuss this in a nice warm restaurant instead of a freezing cold park?"

"Let me ask you," I said. "Did Robert get any provisions at all in Omar's will?"

He crossed his arms in a gesture of impatience.

"No, and he wouldn't have expected any. He was no relation to Omar."

"Would you say, as Omar's personal assistant, that he knew what was in the will?"

"As I've already said," David said, his voice showing his irritation.

"Right. So, Robert knew Guy was to inherit and he probably also knew that Guy was Omar's biological son, so he knew the will wouldn't need to be overturned."

"What are you driving at?"

"What if Guy's murder wasn't about the money? What if we've been looking at it all wrong all along?"

"But why else would Guy have been killed if not for the fortune he'd just inherited?"

"Jealousy, for one. Resentment for a good runner-up. I've got two people who've hinted that Omar tended to ignore

Robert's efforts and give credit to Guy when everyone knew it was undeserved."

"That's a pretty weak argument to accuse someone of a double homicide!"

"I also found out that Robert was brought up in foster care. Only he told me he had a good relationship with his father."

"A lot of people lie about their families! It doesn't mean they're killers."

I felt a headache coming on and I was definitely going to tie David for who was more impatient at the moment.

"Robert slept with Pomme at least once," I said. "She's so slack with the truth that it could even have been more than that. What if Pomme meant more to Robert than he wants us to believe? What if in fact he was wildly incensed about Guy assaulting her?"

"You think Robert killed Guy out of chivalry?"

"I'd say it was more jealousy," I said, looking up at the building. I'd already figured out which windows belonged to Robert's apartment. "Although frankly, it was probably a lot of things that might have been building up over the years and culminated in a single moment that was the tipping point for him."

When David still didn't respond, I blew out a noise of exasperation.

"Look, all I want you to do is play a very small part in a play tonight," I said. "If it works, you free two women to go home to their children for Christmas. If it doesn't, you mildly piss off one low-level administrative flunky whose word wouldn't amount to a pile of day-old *palmiers* against yours."

"I don't like the sound of this."

"I know you don't, and I have to say I'm duly impressed

by your honor and passion for the truth. But tonight, that sense of honor might just stand in the way of two women—"

"Yes, yes, I know—who need to get home to their children."

He made a face that I'm very familiar with. It's an expression of capitulation in the throes of not liking it one bit. I've seen the same expression on Jean-Marc's face many times.

"So, will you do it?"

"A part in a play, you say?"

"That's all. Nothing illegal, I promise."

He sighed and let out an expulsion of cold air that fogged the air between us.

"Okay," he said. "What do you want me to do?"

27

S ince there was a very real danger that Robert might come out to walk his dog, I maneuvered David over to the side of the building near a tall rosebush. We could watch the entrance to the building from here.

"Okay, I said. First you knock on his apartment door and introduce yourself."

David frowned. "So far so good."

"Then you ask if you can come in. Say that Omar left something for Robert in a codicil to the will but you're to give it to him personally."

"That makes no sense. Why would a public defender know anything about Omar Blanchet's will?"

"It doesn't matter," I said patiently. "Robert won't wonder why you're telling him about it. He'll be too curious to see what it's about to think it might be false."

"You appear to have some experience in misrepresenting yourself," he said stiffly.

"Then, when you're inside, you tell him you're visiting him as a courtesy since you're Pomme Toussaint's attorney."

"Okay," he said with a doubtful expression.

"That's when you tell him his prints were found on the knife that killed Cherise."

David gasped. "But that's not true!"

"I know. It's a bluff. It will push him to either deny the charge or vigorously defend his actions. Since I now don't think money had a role to play in Guy or Cherise's death, I'm voting it'll be the latter. He'll want to explain to you how he was sinned against."

"You think he's going to confess to murder?"

"I think there's a good chance. People like Robert aren't used to lying to the police or other figures of authority— that would be you, by the way—and it's also why you're the best person to confront him. As a woman, I wouldn't have nearly the same effect."

"But this is absurd!"

"Yes, very possibly! In which case, you leave, and we are none the worse. But if there's even a chance that Robert unburdens himself and confesses, isn't it worth taking that chance?"

"And you're sure he'll either confess or deny it? Nothing in between?"

"Are you asking me if this is dangerous?"

I waited while he looked at me. I hated to say that because in effect I'd suggested he might be considered cowardly if he didn't do it. I hate many of the things I do in the process of doing the right thing.

"No," he said, finally and took in a long breath before letting it out. "*There appears to be a codicil. May I come in? And by the way your prints were on the knife that killed Cherise.*"

"You got it. Now, let me have your phone."

He pulled out his phone and handed it to me.

"Normally, I'd set this to record but in this case, I'll connect it to my phone instead so I can hear what's going on." I called his number and clicked *Accept* when it rang and then dropped it into his coat pocket.

I put my hand on his shoulder.

"Please remember what incredible good the next few minutes might end up doing for both Liesel and Pomme—no matter how awkward they might potentially feel to you."

"Sure," he said as he straightened his collar and turned toward the building.

I watched him go and realized that in the process of possibly catching a killer, I had in all likelihood just destroyed my chances of a further relationship with David.

I stayed where I was and listened on my phone to the sound of David's steps as they echoed in the tiled foyer of Robert's building until they came to a stop. Then came the knocking on the door and finally the sound of a door creaking open.

"Can I help you?" Robert said.

"Yes, I hope so," David said, his voice strained and barely audible. I prayed he'd speak up. Even having never met him before Robert was sure to realize he was acting strangely.

I heard the sound of Robert's dog barking.

"Hush, Gigi," Robert said.

"My name is David Fontaine. I'm a lawyer for Omar Blanchet. There was a codicil to Monsieur Blanchet's will that appears to involve you. May I come in?"

I held my breath as I listened until Robert finally spoke.

"Yes, Monsieur...what is your name again?"

I didn't love that. I had been counting on Robert being so distracted by the fact that he might be mentioned in

Omar's will that he wouldn't ask questions about David's credentials.

"David Fontaine," David said in that same squeaky voice that broadcasted to the world that he was nervous or lying or both. "This is a very nice apartment."

Don't go off script!

I heard the front door close behind him and something shuffled—probably inside David's pocket—before anyone spoke again.

"The codicil was a surprise to all on Monsieur Blanchet's account," David said.

Don't improvise! Just hit him with the big accusation!

"I know all of Monsieur Blanchet's legal team," Robert said. "I've never heard of you."

I ground my teeth in anguish as I waited to see how David would respond. I wish we'd rehearsed all possible scenarios beforehand but there had just been no time.

"I was hired by Mademoiselle Blanchet," David said. "She was in the process of firing all of the old legal team."

That was actually a pretty good save. I allowed myself to take a breath.

Now quit fooling around and tell him about his prints.

"Do you have a copy of this codicil?" Robert asked.

"No, but I have a question about how your fingerprints ended up on the murder weapon that killed my client Cherise Blanchet."

My stomach tightened. He'd gotten the words out but in such a roundabout way, that I wasn't sure Robert would get what he was saying. Why couldn't he just have blurted it out like we practiced?

"That's impossible," Robert said and I felt my hopes for him blurting out the truth began to ebb away. If he wasn't shocked or badgered into telling the truth we had no hope of getting a confession out of him.

"You are doubting forensic DNA found in a police lab?" David said.

I had to hand it to him. He wasn't ready to give up.

"I am," Robert said in a low voice, "since I know I scrubbed that knife handle to within an inch of it being in factory condition!"

28

I should have been more prepared for Robert's abrupt admission of guilt—it was after all the intended result of this whole gambit. But I'd already wrapped my head around the idea that we'd failed tonight so that when Robert said *he'd wiped the knife* it took me precious seconds to realize what had just happened.

Robert just confessed to killing Cherise!

I was so excited about what I'd heard that I totally missed the next few seconds of conversation, until I heard David cry out and the sound of his phone hitting the floor with an ear-splitting thud.

A sudden spasm of coldness hit my core. I froze for a moment. I literally stood there, my phone in my hand, torn about what to do. Then I ran from my hiding place on the side of the building and called the police.

"My child's been grabbed!" I said into the phone. "Please hurry! I'm at rue de Varenne near rue du Bac. The man is still here! Help!"

I had to assume that anything less than an attempted kidnapping would not result in the kind of immediate response I needed. I'd apologize later. When I glanced at my screen, my stomach dropped when I saw that it wasn't going to matter anyway. The call had failed .

I didn't have time to try again. Cursing my bad luck, I turned and slipped through the front door. I ran up the stairs, my heart pounding and prayed that Robert wasn't finishing David off. When I reached Robert's apartment, I didn't hesitate or knock. I just let myself in, while I put my phone into video mode. I held my phone up and opened the door. The door only opened a few inches.

It was being blocked by the body of a six-foot-two French solicitor. I rammed my shoulder against the door and made a big enough opening to squeeze through. Robert was kneeling over David. And he was holding a fire poker.

Instantly my mind ran to what he must be attempting to do—create a plausible explanation for why David was unconscious—soon to be dead by blunt force trauma. He looked up at me, his face registering his indecision and shock.

"Don't even think of it," I said, holding my phone out to capture the video of Robert bending over David's body on the floor.

The survival instinct must have run pretty deep—years of foster care no doubt—because he leaped to his feet and swung the poker at my hand holding the phone.

Pain roared up into my brain and somewhere in the back of my brain I heard my phone clatter across the floor. I held my throbbing hand to my chest and attempted to back away.

"The police are on their way," I said, my voice a series of terrified, pained gasps.

A look came over Robert's face that was like something out of a bad horror movie. It was something I would've expected Hannibal Lecter to do. It was a look that told me no amount of talking was going to reason with him.

"You!" he said, hefting the fire poker in his hand. "So, it was a lie. My prints weren't found on the knife. Only Madame Blanchet's."

I thought how absurd it was that after everything that had happened, Robert was still calling Liesel by her formal title.

"Look," I said. "It's over, Robert. The cops know everything."

"Move away from the door," he said.

When I didn't, he raised the poker directly over David's head.

"Okay, okay!" I said and stepped away from my only escape access. "Listen to me. You can't explain this away." I pointed to David's body on the floor. "Monsieur Fontaine is a respected member of the French legal profession."

"He broke into my apartment and assaulted me in my own home," Robert said. "I was protecting myself."

"No one will believe you over him."

"He won't get the chance to speak if he's dead. I have a registered gun for this very occasion—home invasion."

My mind whirled trying to think of what to say next, what to do next.

"And me?" I asked. "How are you going to explain it if I don't walk out of here alive?"

"I'll tell them it was an unfortunate misunderstanding," he said with a shrug. "I'll say I was so afraid for my life after clubbing my assailant that I ran to get my gun and when you showed up, I shot you thinking you were one of his confederates."

"You've got it all figured out, don't you?" I said, wondering if there was any chance the police would buy that story.

"I do, and you can stop pretending there's a way out for you. I know the cops aren't coming. If you'd really called them, I'd be hearing the sirens by now. I need you to stand right there."

He motioned to a spot in front of the door. Slowly, I moved to it. I scanned his living room. He'd put up a Christmas tree on a low table decorated with candies and ornaments. It will always amaze me how psychotic people can pretend to be normal in so many ways. When I saw the tree hanging with chocolates and candy canes, I could envision Robert—inveterate psychopath and murderer—shopping at Monoprix or the specialty candy shops to select just the right candies for his tree.

"The cops know you killed Guy," I said.

"More fingerprints on the gun that belong to me?" he said sarcastically. "I don't think so. The police don't know anything."

"Don't you care that Pomme is being held for a crime you committed? Does she mean nothing to you?"

"Shut up!" he said, waving the poker at me.

"Why did you kill Guy? For what possible reason?"

He grinned then, looking almost childlike, his eyes lighting up with excitement. He desperately wanted to tell me. It was all very good to get away with murder—twice—but he wanted someone to know how clever he'd been.

As if he was as normal as the rest of us.

"I killed him for the best possible reason," he said. "For honor and for love." He rubbed the back of his neck and then dragged the hand not holding the poker through his hair.

"When I found out Guy wasn't going to be held accountable for attacking Pomme, I started following him. I saw him pull a gun on Pomme at the Christmas market kiosk! That's when I knew my moment had come. It was so clear to me. When he and Pomme ran off I went after him and intercepted him. I wanted him to see my face."

"And then you shot him," I said.

He leaned against the kitchen counter and crossed his ankles in a relaxed stance. I could see how satisfied he was with himself.

"And the best part?" he continued. "Guy was going to inherit over five-hundred thousand euros. I mean, there was a line a mile long of people who wanted him dead for their own financial reasons. Nobody would suspect me since I didn't stand to inherit anything from his death."

"What about Cherise?" I said, forcing myself not to look at David on the floor at my feet, looking for some signs that he was still breathing, or my phone smashed to plastic shards beside him.

"That worked out rather well, too," he said with a nod. "I

went to her place that night intending to join ranks with her. When I got there, I heard a bunch of screaming coming from her apartment. I hid in the shadows in the hallway and the door opened and who should come out, but Liesel Blanchet."

Things were starting to click into place as Robert spoke. And none of it was good.

"Right then, one of Cherise's neighbors stuck her nose out of her door. She didn't see me but she definitely saw Liesel. Once Liesel was gone and the old biddy went back inside, I knocked on Cherise's door."

I nearly groaned in frustration. It explained why Madame Mordot had seen Liesel but no one else. Certainly not a man skulking in the shadows.

"I couldn't wait to tell Cherise how happy I was that she would inherit all the money and how we could be a team. I could see she was still upset by whatever she and Liesel had been arguing about. She did not look at all happy to see me. But I was so intent on telling her how great things were going to be, I didn't see that something was off with her."

"How so?"

"She was just standing there with her arms crossed, glaring at me. Like *I* was the problem! Instead of the reason she was now going to inherit her father's money free and clear."

"But she didn't know that," I said. "Since she thought Pomme killed Guy."

He snorted in contempt.

"I asked her if she could put in a good word for me with Mo Allard. I came this close to saying that it was because of *me* that she was going to get all the money, ungrateful little bitch! She just looked at me like I was some kind of bug under her shoe. She told me she always thought I was the weak link in her father's business and that she intended to take a more hands-on approach to the operation and firing me was her first task! Can you believe that?"

"So you killed her."

"It's what she deserved. She was no better than her father."

"I thought Omar treated you like a son?"

"He treated me like dirt. Cherise knew it. Everyone knew it."

I knew I was stalling for a miracle or some sign or opportunity to act. I'd been smart enough to put my Taser in my coat pocket but stupidly buttoned the pocket as was my general habit being mindful of pick pockets. By the time I got the button undone and slipped my hand in my pocket, Robert would have plenty of time to brain me with the poker.

"Why do you hate Pomme?" I asked.

"What are you talking about? I love Pomme!"

"And yet she's in jail because of you."

Robert looked uncomfortable.

"That's on her. She deserved what happened to her for sleeping with every man in a five-kilometer radius!" He blew out a noisy breath. "Enough talking."

He moved to the kitchen and began pulling open drawers. A chill fluttered through me as I realized he was looking for the gun he intended to use to execute me and David.

"You're crazy if you think the cops won't suspect you of murder tonight," I said. "Finding two bodies in your apartment will make them go over everything they think they know about you."

"It doesn't matter," he said, raking open a kitchen drawer and pulling out a gun. "I can't let you just leave. You'd tell what you know." He looked at me. "Unless you promise not to?"

I glared at him and he laughed.

"I didn't think so."

"How did the gun you used to kill Guy end up at Cherise's apartment?" I asked hurriedly.

"Isn't the real question *how did they find her fingerprints on the gun*?" he grinned proudly.

"What they found was a clumsy attempt to wrap a dead woman's fingers around a gun handle. Within an hour of the murder, they knew it was fake."

Robert blushed angrily and walked around the other side of the counter to face me. He didn't like being made to look foolish.

"My question," I said, "was how did the gun you used on Guy get to be at Cherise's apartment?"

He faced me and again, more intent on explaining himself and his actions then killing me immediately.

"I figured the safest place for that gun was on my person," he said with a self-satisfied shrug.

I dearly wished my phone was not broken and that the record function was on, but as it was, if I was going to use Robert's confession against him, I was going to have to survive the night first.

"So, when the opportunity presented itself," he continued, "I put Cherise's prints on the gun and left it on a shelf in her living room. Of everyone, Cherise had the biggest motive for wanting Guy dead. I figured the cops would think so too. Plus, I thought it might get Pomme out of jail in time for Christmas."

He looked so proud of himself. I realized he was looking for me to praise him for being such a great guy. But since I knew he intended to kill me tonight, I wasn't really in the mood.

"So, let me get this straight," I said, still stalling for that miracle. "You killed Guy, then you pinned the evidence on Cherise in order to take the blame off Pomme. But you killed Cherise hoping the cops would think it was Liesel. Is that right? So what did Liesel ever do to you?"

He made a face.

"Nothing. Except treat me like I didn't exist. Once I saw she was there at Cherise's that night—and all the screaming? I knew she was going to be the cops' prime suspect. I even had a witness to prove it! Besides, who else but Madame Blanchet had a bigger motive for wanting Cherise dead?" He barked out an ugly laugh.

"I have to say I didn't expect them to find Liesel's prints on the knife that I used! Talk about Christmas coming early!" He laughed again.

"But enough talk," he said as he steadied his hand as he pointed the gun downward at his feet.

At David's head.

"And your own prints?" I said desperately. "Why weren't they on the knife? That's what I don't understand."

He hesitated and then turned to me, instantly re-engaged in recounting his brilliance to the one person he could tell.

And the one person who wouldn't live to tell what she knew.

"I pulled on dishwashing gloves from under her sink," he said proudly, thrusting his chest out. "Pretty clever, huh? Cherise never even suspected. I asked her for a glass of water, and she waved me toward the kitchen like she was some sort of royalty and couldn't be bothered to get it for me. I saw the knife sticking up out of the counter and everything just fell together. I found gloves under the sink, put them on and pulled the knife out of the chopping block. Pretty smart, huh?"

"Or pretty dumb on the part of the police."

That was a calculated risk. Robert could either try to

prove his point to me of how brilliant he was, or just shoot me and win the argument without wasting his breath.

I was betting my life—and David's—that he was the kind of sociopath who needed the last word.

"Ask the police if they think it's dumb!" he shouted. "They walked right into it and picked up every clue I laid out for them! Every single one!"

Out of the corner of my eye I saw the dog sniffing at something on the floor in the living room. Psychopaths could often affect a normalcy and maybe in some cases they could actually be as normal as the rest of us. Even if only for short periods of time. I had one chance and one chance only.

I shot my arm out to point at his Christmas tree in the living room.

"Your dog is eating chocolate!" I screamed.

Robert snapped his head around and then bounded into the Christmas tree to grab his dog by the collar who had been sitting calmly on the floor.

"Gigi, no!" he said. "Bad dog!"

I had my coat button undone and the Taser in my hands in the two steps it took to run after Robert. By the time he turned to face me, I was close enough to jam the nozzle into his neck and let fly a fifty-thousand-volt pulse straight into him.

Ten minutes later I was still sitting on the floor, changing out my Taser cartridge and risking Robert having a massive coronary as I zapped him—two more times whenever I saw him begin to recover—until my Taser ran out of charge. I'd stopped only long enough to fish David's cellphone out of his pocket and call the police.

As I watched Robert out of the corner of my eye as he writhed on the floor, I collected his dropped gun and checked that there were enough bullets in the magazine to defend myself should he somehow manage to pull himself together before the police came.

David was already groaning by this time and starting to come to. I scooted over next to him, keeping one eye on Robert who continued to convulse. The dog was watching her master by cocking her head, as if to better understand what he was doing, but I couldn't detect any real concern on the animal's part.

In my experience dogs are incredibly intuitive about people. Abused dogs may love their abusers but I think they draw the line at crazy.

When I called her over to me, she came immediately, tail wagging.

By this time, David was finding his way onto his hands and knees.

"What the hell happened?" he croaked, looking around the room, his eyes on Robert who continued to convulse.

"He confessed to killing Guy and also Cherise," I said.

David eased himself against the wall and felt the back of his head with his hand. He pulled away fingers that were stained bright red.

"So, the plan worked," he said,

Stepping over Robert, I went to find a kitchen towel which I then wrapped around David's head.

"You'll have to go to the hospital," I said. "They have this whole protocol for possible concussions."

He grunted. "Sounds like you've been down this road before."

"Once or twice."

The sound of police sirens came to us then through the closed windows. Robert had finally stopped spazzing and was lying quietly, his eyes open and blinking. I made sure I had a good grip on the gun. Crazy people were wily. Just when you thought they were out for the count they shot up from the bathtub of cold water with a butcher knife in their hands. That's a very old pop cultural reference but one I still pay particular heed to. I'm pretty sure it'll save my life one day.

"Good work, counselor," I said. "You've got two clients who are going to get to spend Christmas with their children because of you."

He reached out to take my hand and gave it a squeeze just as we heard the noise of what sounded like a squadron of water buffalo thundering up the stairs.

Merry Christmas to all, I thought as I closed my eyes for a split second of peace before the police arrived.

And definitely goodwill toward men.

Most of them, anyway.

Two days later, Christmas morning exploded upon my living room the way it always does when you have children in the scenario. Gone were the calm, contemplative Christmas mornings of my recent past where a cup of coffee and a ruminating moment of introspection and prayer as I gazed out my snow-framed window was the beginning to this sacred day.

This year, I sat down on the couch which was already swamped with ripped Christmas wrapping paper and bows —one of which was stuck to Izzy's head—and watched Robbie play with his presents—most of which were much nosier than I'd realized—while Maddie played with her feet, succeeding in throwing a sock off the couch to Izzy's delight.

Geneviève had come upstairs to my apartment for the festivities and planned on going back down for a nap before our Christmas lunch. I'd invited David for the meal but he left town to spend the holidays with his family.

Both Liesel and Pomme had been released from their incarcerations, and their children returned them. I was especially gratified to hear that Liesel's ex had dragged his feet so much on picking up the girls, that Liesel was able to be reunited with them before he arrived.

While I was sorry that David didn't join us for Christmas lunch—Robbie especially had become very fond of him—I have to say a bigger part of me was glad it was just us for the day.

As much as I enjoyed spending time with David, I have to say the last few days did more to underscore for me that I'd rather be alone than with someone who wasn't a perfect fit. I know that's not realistic and maybe it's an age thing. But it's how I feel.

At my age, I want my relationships alternately stimulating and comfortable and frankly, I prefer expectations of me to be low. Whatever I'd felt for David—or hadn't, as it turned out—in the end, it wasn't me that pulled the plug on us. I don't know whether it was me nearly getting him killed that night or just bossing him in general, but he very smoothly let it be known he was taking himself off the market. On the other hand, he did take possession of Robert's dog, Gigi, so I'm putting my episode with David solidly in the Win column. Especially since I would've had to take her myself if he hadn't. And with two kids and one dog I have my hands full.

Geneviève sat down beside me and handed me a spiked egg nog which I took gratefully.

"A good Christmas for all, *chérie*?" Geneviève said as she gazed out over my wreck of a living room and at least one insanely happy child.

I knew she was also referring to how things had turned out for Pomme and Liesel. Pomme had actually called me to thank me which surprised me greatly and made me feel a little ashamed for how I'd judged her. In the end, I'm glad it didn't alter my actions in the matter. I did what was right regardless of my judgement of her. But I *had* struggled to get to the point of realizing that Pomme's promiscuity— although certainly a reason why a husband might leave— didn't make her an unfit mother or a bad person.

"A wonderful Christmas," I agreed.

In a few hours I'd get Robbie dressed for services at our neighborhood church, Église Saint-Augustin, and Geneviève would mind the baby for me. Later, I'd take everyone, Izzy included, out to the park. It would be busy today of all days with so many little Parisian children trying out their new sleds, but it would also be that much more festive. Plus, it would make that hot mulled wine all the tastier on our cold walk home. Unlike Monoprix or the *boulangeries*, the *Marchés de Noel* would all be open.

As I leaned back into the couch, totally relaxed for the first time since Thanksgiving, I heard my phone ding indicating I'd received a text. I was half tempted not to answer it but since there was at least a small chance it might be from Catherine, I got up to get it.

"Who is it, *chérie*?" Geneviève asked.

<Joyeux Noël, Claire. I am sorry about last time. Do you think we could try again after the holidays?>

I felt a warmth infuse me as I re-read the text.

"It's from Jean-Marc," I said to Geneviève. "Wishing me a happy Christmas."

"Oh, that's nice," she said.

I typed in a thumbs up emoji and sent the text before turning to the kitchen to get started on Christmas morning pancakes when there was a knock at the door. I frowned. Who in the world would be visiting on Christmas morning?

"Are you expecting anyone?" I asked Geneviève.

She didn't answer, just looked expectantly at the door. I

went to the door and opened it and then gasped as my grandson Cameron flew into my arms.

"Merry Christmas, Grammy!" he said happily.

"My darling!" I said, overwhelmed with joy.

Behind him stood his mother, her hand on the handle of her rolling bag, her face pinched, her chin held high.

"Catherine, darling!" I said as Cameron pushed past me into the living room.

"Mother," she responded stonily as she stepped into my apartment. "I believe you have something of mine?"

∼

The saga of Claire, Robbie, Catherine and Baby Maddie continues in *Deadly Adieu, Book 10 of The Claire Baskerville Mysteries.*

Printed in Great Britain
by Amazon